"Hey!"

Laughing, she pushed against his shoulder. "Shove over." The movement cost Gennie a few more precious inches of mattress.

No response.

You're a romantic devil, Gennie thought wryly. Pressing her lips to that unbudgeable shoulder, she slipped out of the bed. Grant immediately took advantage of all the available space.

A loner, Gennie thought, studying him as he lay crosswise over the twisted sheets. He wasn't a man used to making room for anyone....

The sound of running water roused him. Barely half-awake, Grant shifted to discover he was alone in bed. Her warmth was still there—on the sheets, on his skin.

He lay steeped in it a moment, not certain why it felt so right. Not trying to reason out the answers.

Dear Reader:

Nora Roberts, Tracy Sinclair, Jeanne Stephens, Carole Halston, Linda Howard. Are these authors familiar to you? We hope so, because they are just a few of our most popular authors who publish with Silhouette Special Edition each and every month. And the Special Edition list is changing to include new writers with fresh stories. It has been said that discovering a new author is like making a new friend. So during these next few months, be sure to look for books by Sandi Shane, Dorothy Glenn and other authors who have just written their first and second Special Editions, stories we hope you enjoy.

Choosing which Special Editions to publish each month is a pleasurable task, but not an easy one. We look for stories that are sophisticated, sensuous, touching, and great love stories, as well. These are the elements that make Silhouette Special Editions more romantic...and unique.

So we hope you'll find this Silhouette Special Edition just that—*Special*—and that the story finds a special place in your heart.

The Editors at Silhouette

SERL-7/85

NORA ROBERTS
One Man's Art

Silhouette Special Edition

Published by Silhouette Books New York

America's Publisher of Contemporary Romance

To Joan Hohl
For the fun of it.

SILHOUETTE BOOKS
300 E. 42nd St., New York, N.Y. 10017

Copyright © 1985 by Nora Roberts

Distributed by Pocket Books

ISBN: 0-373-09259-8

First Silhouette Books printing September 1985

10 9 8 7 6 5 4 3 2 1

America's Publisher of Contemporary Romance

Printed in the U.S.A.

Books by Nora Roberts

NORA ROBERTS

lives with her two sons in the Blue Ridge Mountains of western Maryland. To be a published author was her lifetime dream, which she has seen fulfilled in the many books that she has written for Silhouette. Renowned for her warm characters and wit, Nora Roberts is a favorite with readers of romance.

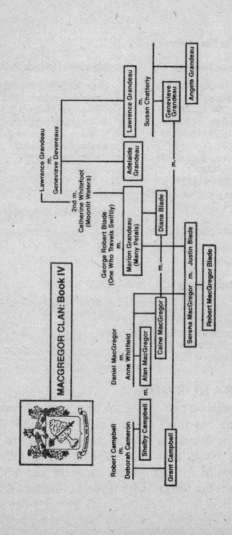

MACGREGOR CLAN: Book IV

Robert Campbell
m.
Deborah Cameron

Shelby Campbell

Grant Campbell

Daniel MacGregor
m.
Anna Whitfield

Alan MacGregor

Caine MacGregor

Serena MacGregor m. Justin Blade

Robert MacGregor Blade

Lawrence Grandeau
m.
Genevieve Devereaux

2nd m.
Catherine Whitefoot
(Moonlit Waters)

George Robert Blade
(One Who Travels Swiftly)
m.
Marion Grandeau
(Many Petals)

Diana Blade

Adelaide Grandeau

Lawrence Grandeau
m.
Susan Chatterly

Genevieve Grandeau

Angela Grandeau

Chapter One

Gennie knew she'd found it the moment she passed the first faded clapboard building. The village, pragmatically and accurately called Windy Point, at last captured her personal expectations for a coastal Maine settlement. She'd found her other stops along the rugged, shifting coastline scenic, picturesque, at times postcard perfect. Perhaps the perfection had been the problem.

When she'd decided on this working vacation, she'd done so with the notion of exploring a different aspect of her talent. Where before, she'd always fancified, mystified, relying on her own bent toward illusions, she'd made a conscious decision to stick to realism, no matter how stark. Indeed, her trunk was laden with her impressions of rock and sea and earth on canvas and sketch pads, but...

There was something more about Windy Point. Or perhaps it was something less. There was no lushness here or soft edges. This was hard country. There were no leafy shade trees, but a few stunted fir and spruce, gnarled and weather-beaten. The road had more than its fair share of bumps.

The village itself, though it wasn't precisely tumbledown, had the air of old age with all its aches and pains. Salt and wind had weathered the buildings, picking away at the paint, scarring the windows. The result wasn't a soft wash, but a toughness.

Gennie saw a functional beauty. There were no frivolous buildings here, no gingerbread. Each building served its purpose—dry goods, post office, pharmacy. The few houses along the main road held that implacable New England practicality in their sturdy shape and tidy size. There might be flowers, adding a surprisingly gay and smiling color against the stern clapboard, but she noted nearly every home had a well-tended vegetable patch at the rear or the side. The petunias might be permitted to grow a bit unruly, but the carrots were tidily weeded.

With her car window down she could smell the village. It smelled quite simply of fish.

She drove straight through first, wanting a complete impression of the main street. She stopped by a churchyard where the granite markers were rather stern and the grass was high and wild, then turned to drive back through again. It wasn't a large town and the road was rather narrow, but she had a sense of spaciousness. You wouldn't bump into your neighbor here unless you meant to. Pleased, Gennie pulled up in front of the dry goods store, guessing this would be the hub of Windy Point's communications network.

The man sitting in an old wooden rocker on the stoop didn't stare, though she knew he'd seen her drive through and backtrack. He continued to rock while he repaired a broken lobster trap. He had the tanned brown face of the coast, guarded eyes, thinning hair, and gnarled strong hands. Gennie promised herself she'd sketch him just like that. She stepped from the car, grabbing her purse as an afterthought, and approached him.

"Hello."

He nodded, his hands still busy with the wooden slats of the trap. "Need some help?"

"Yes." She smiled, enjoying the slow, thick drawl that somehow implied briskness. "Perhaps you can tell me where I can rent a room or a cottage for a few weeks."

The shopkeeper continued to rock while he summed her up with shrewd, faded eyes. City, he concluded, not altogether disdainfully. And South. Though he was a man who considered Boston South, he pegged her as someone who belonged in the humid regions below the Mason-Dixon line. She was neat and pretty enough, though he felt her dark complexion and light eyes had a substantially foreign look. Then again, if you went much farther south than Portland, you were talking foreign.

While he rocked and deliberated, Gennie waited patiently, her rich black hair lifting from her shoulders and blowing back in the salt-scented breeze. Her experience in New England during the past few months had taught her that while most people were fair-minded and friendly enough, they generally took their time about it.

Didn't look like a tourist, he thought—more like one of those fairy princesses his granddaughter read about in her picture books. The delicate face came to a subtle point at the chin and the sweep of cheekbones added hauteur. Yet she smiled, softening the look, and her eyes were the color of the sea.

"Don't get many summer people," he said at length. "All gone now anyhow."

He wouldn't ask, Gennie knew. But she could be expansive when it suited her purpose. "I don't think I qualify as summer people, Mr...."

"Fairfield—Joshua Fairfield."

"Geneviève Grandeau." She offered a hand which he found satisfactorily firm in his work-roughened one. "I'm an artist. I'd like to spend some time here painting."

An artist, he mused. Not that he didn't like pictures, but he wasn't sure he completely trusted the people who produced them. Drawing was a nice hobby, but for a job...still, she had a good smile and she didn't slouch. "Might be there's a cottage 'bout two miles out. Widow Lawrence ain't sold it yet." The chair creaked as he moved back and forth. "Could be she'll rent it for a time."

"It sounds good. Where can I reach her?"

"'Cross the road, at the post office." He rocked for another few seconds. "Tell her I sent you over," he decided.

Gennie gave him a quick grin. "Thank you, Mr. Fairfield."

The post office was hardly more than a counter and four walls. One of the walls was taken up with slots where a woman in a dark cotton dress deftly sorted mail. She even *looks* like a Widow Lawrence, Gennie thought with inner pleasure as she noted the neat circular braid at the back of the woman's head.

"Excuse me."

The woman turned, giving Gennie a quick, birdlike glance before she came over to the counter. "Help you?"

"I hope so. Mrs. Lawrence?"

"Ayah."

"Mr. Fairfield told me you might have a cottage to rent."

The small mouth pursed—the only sign of facial movement. "I've a cottage for sale."

"Yes, he explained that." Gennie tried her smile again. She wanted the town—and the two miles distance from it the cottage would give her. "I wonder if you'd consider renting it for a few weeks. I can give you references if you'd like."

Mrs. Lawrence studied Gennie with cool eyes. She made her own references. "For how long?"

"A month, six weeks."

She glanced down at Gennie's hands. There was an intricate gold twist of a ring, but it was on the wrong finger. "Are you alone?"

"Yes." Gennie smiled again. "I'm not married, Mrs. Lawrence. I've been traveling through New England for several months, painting. I'd like to spend some time here at Windy Point."

"Painting?" the widow finished with another long look.

"Yes."

Mrs. Lawrence decided she liked Gennie's looks— and that she was a young woman who didn't run on endlessly about herself. And fact was fact. An empty cottage was a useless thing. "The place is clean and the plumbing's good. Roof was fixed two years back, but the stove's got a temperament of its own. There's two bedrooms but one of 'em stands empty.''

This is painful for her, Gennie realized, though the widow's voice stayed even and her eyes were steady. She's thinking about all the years she lived there.

"Got no close neighbors, and the phone's been taken out. Could be you could have one put in if you've a mind to.''

"It sounds perfect, Mrs. Lawrence.''

Something in Gennie's tone made the woman clear her throat. It had been sympathy and understanding quietly offered. After a moment she named a sum for the month's rent far more reasonable than Gennie had expected. Characteristically she didn't hesitate, but went with her instincts.

"I'll take it.''

The first faint flutter of surprise showed on the widow's face. "Without seeing it?''

"I don't need to see it.'' With a brisk practicality Mrs. Lawrence admired, Gennie pulled a checkbook out of her purse and dashed off the amount. "Maybe you can tell me what I'll need in the way of linen and dishes.''

Mrs. Lawrence took the check and studied it. "Genevieve,'' she murmured.

"Genviève,'' Gennie corrected, flowing easily over the French. "After my grandmother.'' She smiled again, softening that rather ruthless fairy look. "Everyone calls me Gennie.''

An hour later Gennie had the keys to the cottage in her purse, two boxes of provisions in the back seat of her car and directions to the cottage in her hand. She'd passed off the distant, wary stares of the villagers and had managed not to chuckle at the open ogling of a scrawny teenager who'd come into the dry goods store while she was mulling over a set of earthenware dishes.

It was dusk by the time she was ready to set out. The clouds were low and unfriendly now, and the wind had picked up. It only added to the sense of adventure. Gennie set out on the narrow, bumpy road that led to the sea with a restless inner excitement that meant something new was on the horizon.

She came by her love of adventure naturally. Her great-great-grandfather had been a pirate—an unapologetic rogue of the sea. His ship had been fast and fierce, and he had taken what he wanted without qualm. One of Gennie's treasures was his logbook. Philippe Grandeau had recorded his misdeeds with flair and a sense of irony she'd never been able to resist. She might have inherited a strong streak of practicality from the displaced aristocrats on her mother's side, but Gennie was honest enough to know she'd have sailed with the pirate Philippe and loved every minute of it.

As her car bounced along the ruts, she took in the scenery, so far removed from her native New Orleans it might have been another planet. This was no place for long lazy days and riotous nights. In this rocky, windswept world, you'd have to be on your toes every minute. Mistakes wouldn't be easily forgiven here.

But she saw more than hard land and rock. Integrity. She sensed it in the land that vied continually with the sea. It knew it would lose, inch by minute inch, century after endless century, but it wasn't giving in. Though the shadows lengthened with evening, she stopped, compelled to put some of her impressions on paper.

There was an inlet some yards from the road, restless now as the storm approached. As Gennie pulled out a sketchbook and pencil, she caught the smell of decaying fish and seaweed. It didn't make her wrinkle her nose; she understood that it was part of the strange lure that called men forever to the sea.

The soil was thin here, the rocks worn smooth. Near the road were clumps of wild blueberry bushes, pregnant with the last of the summer fruit. She could hear the wind—a distinctly feminine sound—sighing and moaning. She couldn't see the sea yet, but she could smell it and taste it in the air that swirled around her.

She had no one to answer to, no timetable to keep. Gennie had long since taken her freedom for granted, but solitude was something else. She felt it here, near the little windswept inlet, along the narrow, impossible road. And she held it to her.

When she was back in New Orleans, a city she loved, and she soaked up one of those steamy days that smelled of the river and humanity, she would remember passing an hour in a cool, lonely spot where she might have been the only living soul for miles.

Relaxed, but with that throb of excitement just buzzing along her skin, she sketched, going into much more detail than she had intended when she'd stopped. The lack of human noises appealed to her. Yes, she was going to enjoy Windy Point and the little cottage very much.

Finished, she tossed her sketchbook back in the car. It was nearly dark now or she might have stayed longer, wandered closer to the water's edge. Long days of painting stretched ahead of her...and who knew what else a month could bring? With a half smile, she turned the key in the ignition.

When she got only a bad-tempered rattle, she tried again. She was rewarded with a wheeze and a groan and a distinctly suspicious clunk. The car had given her a bit of trouble in Bath, but the mechanic there had tightened this and fiddled with that. It had been running like a top ever since. Thinking of the jolting road, Gennie decided that what could be tightened could just as easily be loosened again. With a mildly annoyed oath, she got out of the car to pop the hood.

Even if she had the proper tools, which she didn't think included the screwdriver and flashlight in her glove compartment, she would hardly know what to do with them. Closing the hood again, she glanced up and down the road. Deserted. The only sound was the wind. It was nearly dark, and by her calculations she was at the halfway point between town and the cottage. If she hiked back, someone was bound to give her a lift, but if she went on she could probably be in the cottage in fifteen minutes. With a shrug, she dug her flashlight out of the glove compartment and did what she usually did. She went forward.

She needed the light almost immediately. The road was no better to walk on than to drive on, but she'd have to take care to keep to it unless she wanted to end up lost or taking a dunking in an inlet. Ruts ran deeply here, rocks worked their way up there, so that she wondered how often anyone actually traveled this stretch.

Darkness fell swiftly, but not in silence. The wind whipped at her hair, keeping up its low, keening sound. There were wisps of fog at her feet now which she hoped would stay thin until she was indoors. Then she forgot the fog as the storm burst out, full of fury.

Under other circumstances, Gennie wouldn't have minded a soaking, but even her sense of adventure was strained in the howling darkness where her flashlight cut a pitiful beam through the slashing rain. Annoyance was her first reaction as she continued to trudge along the uneven road in thoroughly wet sneakers. Gradually annoyance became discomfort and discomfort, unease.

A flash of lightning would illuminate a cropping of rocks or stunted bush, throwing hard, unfriendly shadows. Even a woman possessing a pedestrian imagination might have had a qualm. Gennie had visions of nasty little elves grinning out of the cloaking darkness. Humming tunelessly to stave off panic, she concentrated on the beam of her flashlight.

So I'm wet, Gennie told herself as she dragged dripping hair out of her eyes. It's not going to kill me. She gave another uneasy glance at the side of the road. There was no dark, Gennie decided, like the dark of the countryside. And where was the cottage? Surely she'd walked more than a mile by now. Halfheartedly she swung the light in a circle. Thunder boiled over her head while the rain slapped at her face. It would take a minor miracle to find a dark, deserted cottage with only the beam of a household flashlight.

Stupid, she called herself while she wrapped her arms tightly around her chest and tried to think. It was always stupid to set out toward the unknown when you had a choice. And yet she would always do so. There seemed to be nothing left but find her way back to the car and wait out the storm there. The prospect of a long wet night in a compact wasn't pleasant, but it had it all over wandering around lost in a thunderstorm. And there was a bag of cookies in the car, she remembered while she continued to stroke the flashlight back and forth, just in case there was—something out there. With a sigh, she gave one last look down the road.

She saw it. Gennie blinked rain out of her eyes and looked again. A light. Surely that was a light up ahead. A light meant shelter, warmth, company. Without hesitation, Gennie headed toward it.

It turned out to be another mile at best, while the storm and the road worsened. Lightning slashed the sky with a wicked purple light, tossing out a brief eerie glow that made the darkness only deeper when it faded. To keep from stumbling, she was forced to move slowly and keep her eyes on the ground. She began to be certain she'd never be dry or warm again. The light up ahead stayed steady and true, helping her to resist glancing over her shoulder too often.

She could hear the sea now, beating violently on rocks and shale. Once in a flash of lightning, she thought she saw the crest of angry waves, white-capped and turbulent in the distance. Even the rain smelled of the sea now—an angry, vengeful one. She wouldn't—couldn't—allow herself to be frightened, though her heart was beating fast from more than the two-mile walk. If she admitted she was frightened, she would give in to the urge to run and would end up over a cliff, in a ditch, or in some soundless vacuum.

The sense of displacement was so great, she might have simply sat on the road and wept had it not been for the steady beam of light sending out the promise of security.

When Gennie saw the silhouette of the building behind the curtain of rain she nearly laughed aloud. A lighthouse—one of those sturdy structures that proved man had some sense of altruism. The guiding light hadn't come from the high revolving lens but from a window. Gennie didn't question, but quickened her pace as much as she dared. Someone was there—a gnarled old man perhaps, a former seaman. He'd have a bottle of rum and talk in brief salty sentences. As a new bolt of lightning slashed across the sky, Gennie decided she already adored him.

The structure seemed huge to her—a symbol of safety for anyone lost and storm-tossed. It looked stunningly white under the play of her flashlight as she searched the base for a door. The window that was lit was high up, the top of three on the side Gennie approached.

She found a door of thick rough wood and beat on it. The violence of the storm swallowed the sound and tossed it away. Nearer to panic than she wanted to admit, Gennie pounded again. Could she have come so far, got so close, and then not be heard? The old keeper was in there, she thought as she beat on the door, probably whistling and whittling, perhaps idling away the evening putting a ship into a bottle.

Desperate, Gennie leaned against the door, feeling the hard, wet wood against her cheek as well as the side of her fist as she continued to thud against it. When the door opened, she went with it, overbalancing. Her arms were gripped hard as she pitched forward.

"Thank God!" she managed. "I was afraid you wouldn't hear me." With one hand she dragged her sopping hair out of her face and looked up at the man she considered her savior.

The one thing he wasn't was old. Nor was he gnarled. Rather he was young and lean, but the narrow, tanned face of planes and angles might have been a seafaring one—in her great-great-grandfather's line. His hair was as dark as hers, and as thick, with that careless windblown effect a man might get if he stood on the point of a ship. His mouth was full and unashamedly sensual, the nose a bit aristocratic in the rugged face. His eyes were a deep, deep brown under dark brows. They weren't friendly, Gennie decided, not even curious. They were simply annoyed.

"How the hell did you get here?"

It wasn't the welcome she had expected, but her trek through the storm had left her a bit muddled. "I walked," she told him.

"Walked?" he repeated. "In this? From where?"

"A couple of miles back—my car stalled." She began to shiver, either with chill or with reaction. He'd yet to release her, and she'd yet to recover enough to demand it.

"What were you doing driving around on a night like this?"

"I—I'm renting Mrs. Lawrence's cottage. My car stalled, then I must have missed the turnoff in the dark. I saw your light." She heaved a long breath and realized abruptly that her legs were shaking. "Can I sit down?"

He stared at her for another minute, then with something like a grunt nudged her toward a sofa. Gennie sank down on it, dropped her head back, and concentrated on pulling herself together.

And what the hell was he supposed to do with her? Grant asked himself. Brows lowered, he stared down at her. At the moment she looked like she'd keel over if he breathed too hard. Her hair was plastered to her head, curling just a bit and dark as the night itself. Her face wasn't fine or delicate, but beautiful in the way of medieval royalty—long bones, sharp features. A Celtic or Gallic princess with a compact athletic little body he could see clearly as her clothes clung to it.

He thought the face and body might be appealing enough, under certain circumstances, but what had thrown him for an instant when she'd looked up at him had been her eyes. Sea green, huge, and faintly slanted. Mermaid's eyes, he'd thought. For a heartbeat, or perhaps only half of that, Grant had wondered if she'd been some mythical creature who'd been tossed ashore in the storm.

Her voice was soft and flowing, and though he recognized it as Deep South, it seemed almost a foreign tongue after the coastal Maine cadence he'd grown used to. He wasn't a man to be pleased with having a magnolia blossom tossed on his doorstep. When she opened her eyes and smiled at him, Grant wished fervently he'd never opened the door.

"I'm sorry," Gennie began, "I was barely coherent, wasn't I? I suppose I wasn't out there for more than an hour, but it seemed like days. I'm Gennie."

Grant hooked his thumbs in the pockets of his jeans and frowned at her again. "Campbell, Grant Campbell."

Since he left it at that and continued to frown, Gennie did her best to pick things up again. "Mr. Campbell, I can't tell you how relieved I was when I saw your light."

He stared down at her another moment, thinking briefly that she looked familiar. "The turnoff for the Lawrence place's a good mile back."

Gennie lifted a brow at the tone. Did he actually expect her to go back outside and stumble around until she found it? She prided herself on being fairly even-tempered for an artist, but she was wet and cold, and Grant's unfriendly, scowling face tripped the last latch. "Look, I'll pay you for a cup of coffee and the use of this—" she thumped a hand on the sofa and a soft plume of dust rose up "—thing for the night."

"I don't take in lodgers."

"And you'd probably kick a sick dog if he got in your way," she added evenly. "But I'm not going back out there tonight, Mr. Campbell, and I wouldn't advise trying to toss me out, either."

That amused him, though the humor didn't show in his face. Nor did he correct her assumption that he had meant to shove her back into the storm. The statement had been simply meant to convey his displeasure and the fact that he wouldn't take her money. If he hadn't been annoyed, he might have appreciated the fact that soaking wet and slightly pale, she held her own.

Without a word he walked over to the far side of the room and crouched to rummage through a scarred oak cabinet. Gennie stared straight ahead, even as she heard the sound of liquid hitting glass.

"You need brandy more than coffee at the moment," Grant told her, and shoved the glass under her nose.

"Thank you," Gennie said in an icy tone southern women are the champions of. She didn't sip, but drank it down in one swallow, letting the warmth shock her system back to normal. Distantly polite, she handed the empty glass back to him.

Grant glanced down at it and very nearly smiled. "Want another?"

"No," she said, frigid and haughty, "thank you."

I have, he mused wryly, been put in my place. Princess to peasant. Considering his option, Grant rocked back on his heels. Through the thick walls of the lighthouse, the storm could be heard whipping and wailing. Even the mile ride to the Lawrence place would be wild and miserable, if not dangerous. It would be less trouble to bed her down where she was than to drive her to the cottage. With an oath that was more weary than pungent he turned away.

"Well, come on," he ordered without looking back, "you can't sit there shivering all night."

Gennie considered—seriously considered—heaving her purse at him.

The staircase charmed her. She nearly made a comment on it before she stopped herself. It was iron and circular, rising up and up the interior. Grant stepped off onto the second level which Gennie calculated was a good twenty feet above the first. He moved like a cat in the dark while she held on to the rail and waited for him to hit the light switch.

It cast a dim glow and many shadows over the bare wood floor. He passed through a door on the right into what she discovered were his sleeping quarters— small, not particularly neat, but with a curvy antique brass bed Gennie fell instantly in love with. Grant went to an old chifforobe that might have been beautiful with refinishing. Muttering to himself, he routed around and unearthed a faded terrycloth robe.

"Shower's across the hall," he said briefly, and dumped the robe in Gennie's arms before he left her alone.

"Thank you very much," she mumbled while his footsteps retreated back down the stairs. Chin high, eyes gleaming, she stalked across the hall and found herself charmed all over again.

The bath was white porcelain and footed with brass fixtures he obviously took the time to polish. The room was barely more than a closet, but somewhere in its history it had been paneled in cedar and lacquered. There was a pedestal sink and a narrow little mirror. The light was above her, operated by a pull string.

Stripping gratefully out of her cold, wet clothes, Gennie stepped into the tub and drew the thin circular curtain. In an instant, she had hot water spraying out of the tiny shower head and warming her body. Gennie was certain paradise could have felt no sweeter, even when it was guarded by the devil.

In the kitchen Grant made a fresh pot of coffee. Then, as an afterthought, he opened a can of soup. He supposed he'd have to feed her. Here, at the back of the tower, the sound of the sea was louder. It was a sound he was used to—not so he no longer heard it, but so he expected to. If it was vicious and threatening as it was tonight, Grant acknowledged it, then went about his business.

Or he would have gone about his business if he hadn't found a drenched woman outside his door. Now he calculated he'd have to put in an extra hour that night to make up for the time she was costing him. With his first annoyance over, Grant admitted it couldn't be helped. He'd give her the basic hospitality of a hot meal and a roof over her head, and that would be that.

A smile lightened his features briefly when he remembered how she had looked at him when she'd sat dripping on his sofa. The lady, he decided, was no pushover. Grant had little patience with pushovers.

When he chose company, he chose the company of people who said what they thought and were willing to stand by it. In a way, that was why Grant was off his self-imposed schedule.

It had barely been a week since his return from Hyannis Port where he'd given away his sister, Shelby, in her marriage to Alan MacGregor. He'd discovered, uncomfortably, that the wedding had made him sentimental. It hadn't been difficult for the MacGregors to persuade him to stay on for an extra couple of days. He'd liked them, blustery old Daniel in particular, and Grant wasn't a man who took to people quickly. Since childhood he'd been cautious, but the MacGregors as a group were irresistible. And he'd been weakened somewhat by the wedding itself.

Giving his sister away, something that would have been his father's place had he lived, had brought such a mix of pain and pleasure that Grant had been grateful to have the distraction of a few days among the MacGregors before he returned to Windy Point—even to the extent of being amused by Daniel's not so subtle probing into his personal life. He'd enjoyed himself enough to accept an open-ended invitation to return. An invitation even he was surprised that he intended to act on.

For now there was work to be done, but he resigned himself that a short interruption wouldn't damage his status quo beyond repair. As long as it remained short. She could bunk down in the spare room for the night, then he'd have her out and away in the morning. He was nearly in an amiable mood by the time the soup started to simmer.

Grant heard her come in, though the noise from outside was still fierce. He turned, prepared to make a moderately friendly comment, when the sight of her in his robe went straight to his gut.

Damn, she was beautiful. Too beautiful for his peace of mind. The robe dwarfed her, though she'd rolled the frayed sleeves nearly to the elbow. The faded blue accented the honey-rich tone of her skin. She'd brushed her damp hair back, leaving her face un-framed but for a few wayward curls that sprung out near her temples. With her eyes pale green and the dark lashes wet, she looked to him more than ever like the mermaid he'd nearly taken her for.

"Sit down," he ordered, furiously annoyed by the flare of unwelcome desire. "You can have some soup."

Gennie paused a moment, her eyes skimming up and down his back before she sat at the rough wooden table. "Why, thank you." His response was an unin-telligible mutter before he thumped a bowl in front of her. She picked up the spoon, not about to let pride get in the way of hunger. Though surprised, she said nothing when he sat opposite her with a bowl of his own.

The kitchen was small and brightly lit and very, very quiet. The only sound came from the wind and rest-less water outside the thick walls. At first Gennie ate with her eyes stubbornly on the bowl in front of her, but as the sharp hunger passed she began to glance around the room. Tiny certainly, but with no wasted space. Rough oak cabinets ringed the walls giving generous room for supplies. The counters were wood as well, but sanded and polished. She saw the modern conveniences of a percolator and a toaster.

He took better care of this room, she decided, than he did the rest of the house. No dishes in the sink, no crumbs or spills. And the only scents were the kitcheny aromas of soup and coffee. The appliances were old and a bit scarred, but they weren't grimy.

As her first hunger ebbed, so did her anger. She had, after all, invaded his privacy. Not everyone offered hospitality to a stranger with smiles and open arms. He had scowled, but he hadn't shut the door in her face. And he had given her something dry to wear and food, she added as she did her best to submerge pride.

With a slight frown she skimmed her gaze over the tabletop until it rested on his hands. Good God, she thought with a jolt, they were beautiful. The wrists were narrow, giving a sense not of weakness but of graceful strength and capability. The backs of his hands were deeply tanned and unmarred, long and lean, as were his fingers. The nails were short and straight. Masculine was her first thought, then delicate came quickly on the tail of it. Gennie could picture the hands holding a flute just as easily as she could see them wielding a saber.

For a moment she forgot the rest of him in her fascination with his hands, and her reaction to them. She felt the stir but didn't suppress it. She was certain any woman who saw those romantic, exquisite hands would automatically wonder just what they would feel like on her skin. Impatient hands, clever. They were the kind that could either rip the clothes off a woman or gently undress her before she had any idea what was happening.

When a thrill Gennie recognized as anticipation sprinted up her spine, she caught herself. What was she thinking of! Even her imagination had no business sneaking off in that direction. A little dazed by the feeling that wouldn't be dismissed, she lifted her gaze to his face.

He was watching her—coolly, like a scientist watching a specimen. When she'd stopped eating so suddenly, he'd seen her eyes go to his hands and remain there with her lashes lowered just enough to conceal their expression. Grant had waited, knowing sooner or later she'd look up. He'd been expecting that icy anger or frosty politeness. The numb shock on her face puzzled him, or more accurately intrigued him. But it was the vulnerability that made him want her almost painfully. Even when she had stumbled into the house, wet and lost, she hadn't looked defenseless. He wondered what she would do if he simply got up, hauled her to her feet and dragged her up into his bed. He wondered what in the hell was getting into him.

They stared at each other, each battered by feelings neither of them wanted while the rain and the wind beat against the walls, separating them from everything civilized. He thought again that she looked like some temptress from the sea. Gennie thought he'd have given her rogue of an ancestor a run for his money.

Grant's chair legs scraped against the floor as he pushed back from the table. Gennie froze.

"There's a room on the second level with a bunk." His eyes were hard and dark with suppressed anger—his stomach knotted with suppressed desire.

Gennie found that her palms were damp with nerves and was infuriated. Better to be infuriated with him. "The couch down here is fine," she said coldly.

He shrugged. "Suit yourself." Without another word, he walked out. Gennie waited until she heard his footsteps on the stairs before she pressed a hand to her stomach. The next time she saw a light in the dark, she told herself, she'd run like hell in the opposite direction.

Chapter Two

Grant hated to be interrupted. He'd tolerate being cursed, threatened or despised, but he never tolerated interruptions. It had never mattered to him particularly if he was liked, as long as he was left alone to do as he chose. He'd grown up watching his father pursue the goodwill of others—a necessary aspect in the career of a senator who had chosen to run for the highest office in the country.

Even as a child Grant knew his father was a man who demanded extreme feelings. He was loved by some, feared or hated by others, and on a campaign trail he could inspire a fierce loyalty. He had been a man who would go out of his way to do a favor— friend or stranger—it had never mattered. His ideals had been high, his memory keen, and his flair for words admirable. Senator Robert Campbell had been a man who had felt it his duty to make himself accessible to the public. Right up to the moment someone had put three bullets into him.

Grant hadn't only blamed the man who had held the gun, or the profession of politics, as his sister had done. In his own way Grant had blamed his father. Robert Campbell had given himself to the world, and it had killed him. Perhaps it was as a direct result that Grant gave himself to no one.

He didn't consider the lighthouse a refuge. It was simply his place. He appreciated the distance it gave him from others, and enjoyed the harshness and the harmony of the elements. If it gave him solitude, it was as necessary to his work as it was to himself. He required the hours, even the days, of aloneness. Uninterrupted thought was something Grant considered his right. No one, absolutely no one, was permitted to tamper with it.

The night before he'd been midway through his current project when Gennie's banging had forced him to stop. Grant was perfectly capable of ignoring a knock on the door, but since it had broken his train of thought, he had gone down to answer—with the idea of strangling the intruder. Gennie might consider herself lucky he'd only resorted to rudeness. A hapless tourist had once found himself faced with an irate Grant, who had threatened to toss him into the ocean.

Since it had taken Grant the better part of an hour after he'd left Gennie in the kitchen to get his mind back on his work, he'd been up most of the night. Interruptions. Intrusions. Intolerable. He'd thought so then, and now as the sun slanted in the window and onto the foot of his bed, he thought so again.

Groggy after what amounted to almost four hours sleep, Grant listened to the voice that drifted up the stairwell. She was singing some catchy little tune you'd hear every time you turned on the radio—something Grant did every day of his life, just as religiously as he turned on the TV and read a dozen newspapers. She sang well, in a low-pitched, drumming voice that turned the cute phrasing into something seductive. Bad enough she'd interrupted his work the night before, now she was interrupting his sleep.

With a pillow over his head, he could block it out. But, he discovered, he couldn't block out his reaction to it. It was much too easy in the dark, with the sheet warm under his chest, to imagine her. Swearing, Grant tossed the pillow aside and got out of bed to pull on a pair of cutoffs. Half asleep, half aroused, he went downstairs.

The afghan she'd used the night before was already neatly folded on the sofa. Grant scowled at it before he followed Gennie's voice into the kitchen.

She was still in his robe, barefoot, with her hair waving luxuriously down her back. He'd like to have touched it to see if those hints of red that seemed to shimmer through the black were really there or just a trick of the light.

Bacon sizzled in a pan on the stove, and the coffee smelled like heaven.

"What the hell are you doing?"

Gennie whirled around clutching a kitchen fork, one hand lifting to her heart in reflex reaction. Despite the discomfort of the sofa, she'd woken in the best of moods—and starving. The sun was shining, gulls were calling, and the refrigerator had been liberally stocked. Gennie had decided Grant Campbell deserved another chance. As she'd puttered in his kitchen, she'd made a vow to be friendly at all costs.

He stood before her now, half naked and obviously angry, his hair sleep-tumbled and a night's growth of beard shadowing his chin. Gennie gave him a determined smile. "I'm making breakfast. I thought it was the least I could do in return for a night's shelter."

Again he had the sensation of something familiar about her he couldn't quite catch. His frown only deepened. "I don't like anyone messing with **my** things."

Gennie opened her mouth, then shut it again before anything nasty could slip out. "The only thing I've broken is an egg," she said mildly as she indicated the bowl of eggs she intended to scramble. "Why don't you do us both a favor? Get a cup of coffee, sit down, and shut up." With an almost imperceptible toss of her head, she turned her back on him.

Grant's brows rose not so much in surprise as in appreciation. Not everyone could tell you to shut up in a butter-melting voice and make it work. He had the feeling he wasn't the first person she'd given the order to. With something perilously close to a grin, he got a mug and did exactly what she said.

She didn't sing anymore as she finished making the meal, but he had the feeling she would've muttered bad-temperedly if she hadn't wanted him to think she was unaffected by him. In fact, he was certain there was a good bit of muttering and cursing going on inside her head.

As he sipped coffee the grogginess gave way to alertness, and hunger. For the first time he sat in the tiny kitchen while a woman fixed his breakfast. Not something he'd want to make a habit of, Grant mused while he watched her—but then again, it wasn't an unpleasant experience.

Still clinging to silence, Gennie set plates on the table, then followed them with a platter of bacon and eggs. "Why were you going to the old Lawrence place?" he asked as he served himself.

Gennie sent him a narrowed-eyed glare. *So now we're going to make polite conversation,* she thought and nearly ground her teeth. "I'm renting it," she said briefly, and dashed salt on her eggs.

"Thought the Widow Lawrence had it up for sale."

"She does."

"You're a little late in the season for renting a beach cottage," Grant commented over a mouthful of eggs.

Gennie gave a quick shrug as she concentrated on her breakfast. "I'm not a tourist."

"No?" He gave her a long steady look she found both deft and intrusive. "Louisiana, isn't it? New Orleans, Baton Rouge?"

"New Orleans." Gennie forgot annoyance long enough to study him in turn. "You're not local, either."

"No," he said simply, and left it at that.

Oh, no, she thought, he wasn't going to start a conversation, then switch it off when it suited him. "Why a lighthouse?" she persisted. "It's not operational, is it? It was the light from the window I followed last night, not the beacon."

"Coast Guard takes care of this stretch with radar. This station hasn't been used in ten years. Did you run out of gas?" he asked before she realized he'd never answered the why.

"No. I'd pulled off the side of the road for a few minutes, then when I tried to start the car again, it just made a few unproductive noises." She shrugged and bit into a slice of bacon. "I guess I'll have to get a tow truck in town."

Grant made a sound that might have been a laugh. "You might get a tow truck up at Bayside, but you're not going to find one at Windy Point. I'll take a look at it," he told her as he finished off his breakfast. "If it's beyond me, you can get Buck Gates from town to come out and get it started."

She studied him for nearly thirty seconds. "Thank you," Gennie said warily.

Grant rose and put his plate in the sink. "Go get dressed," he ordered. "I've got work to do." For the second time he left Gennie alone in the kitchen.

Just once, she thought as she stacked her plate on top of his, she'd like to get in the last word. Giving the belt of Grant's robe a quick tug, she started out of the room. Yes, she'd go get dressed, Gennie told herself. And she'd do it quickly before he changed his mind. Rude or not, she'd accept his offer of help. Then as far as she was concerned, Grant Campbell could go to the devil.

There wasn't any sign of him on the second floor when she slipped into the bathroom to change. Gennie stripped out of the robe and hung it on a hook on the back of the door. Her clothes were dry, and she thought she could ignore the fact that her tennis shoes were still a bit cold and damp. With luck she could be settled into the cottage within the hour. That should leave her the best of the afternoon for sketching. The idea kept Gennie's spirits high as she made her way back downstairs. Again there was no sign of Grant. After a brief fight with the heavy front door, Gennie went outside.

It was so clear she nearly caught her breath. Whatever fog or fury had visited that place the night before had been swept clean. The places on the earth where the air really sparkled were rare, she knew, and this was one of them. The sky was blue and cloudless, shot through with the yellow light of the sun. There was some grass on this side of the lighthouse, tough and as wild as the few hardy flowers that were scattered through it. Goldenrod swayed in the breeze announcing the end of summer, but the sun shone hotly.

She could see the narrow rut of a road she'd traveled on the night before, but was surprised by the three-story farmhouse only a few hundred yards away. That it was deserted was obvious by the film of dirt on the windows and the waist-high grass, but it wasn't dilapidated. It would have belonged to the keeper and his family, Gennie concluded, when the lighthouse was still functional. They would have had a garden and perhaps a few chickens. And there would have been nights when the wind howled and the waves crashed that the keeper would have stayed at his station while his family sat alone and listened.

The white paint was faded, but the shutters hung true. She thought it sat on its hill waiting to be filled again.

There was a sturdy little pickup near the base of the slope which she assumed was Grant's. Because he was nowhere in sight, Gennie wandered around the side of the lighthouse, answering the call of the sea.

This time Gennie did catch her breath. She could see for miles, down the irregular coastline, over to tiny islands, and out to the distant horizon. There were boats on the water, staunch, competent little boats of the lobstermen. She knew she would see no chrome and mahogany crafts here, nor should she. This was a place of purpose, not idle pleasure. Strength, durability. That's what she felt as she looked out into blue-green water that frothed white as it flung itself at the rocks.

Seaweed floated in the surf, gathering and spreading with the movement of the water. The sea had its way with everything here. The rocks were worn smooth by it, and the ledges rose showing colors from gray to green with a few muted streaks of orange. Shells littered the shoreline, flung out by the sea and yet to be trampled under a careless foot. The smell of salt and fish was strong. She could hear the toll of the bell buoys, the hollow hoot of the whistling markers, the distant putter of the lobster boats and the mournful cry of gulls. There was nothing, no sound, no sight, no smell, that came from anything other than that endless, timeless sea.

Gennie felt it—the pull, the tug that had called men and women to it from the dawn of time. If humanity had truly sprung from there, perhaps that was why they were so easily lured back to it. She stood on the ledge above the narrow, rocky beach and lost herself in it. Danger, challenge, peace; she felt them all and was content.

She didn't hear Grant come behind her. Gennie was too caught up in the sea itself to sense him, though he watched her as a minute stretched to two and two into three. She looked right there, he thought and could have cursed her for it. The land was his, this small, secluded edge of land that hovered over the sea.

He wouldn't claim to own the sea, not even when it rose high at noon to lick at the verge of his land, but this slice of rock and wild grass belonged to him, exclusively. She had no right to look as though she belonged—to make him wonder if the cliff would ever be only his again.

The wind plastered her clothes against her, as the rain had done the night before, accenting her slim, athletic body with its woman's roundness. Her hair danced frantically and free while the sun teased out those touches of fire in the ebony that seemed to hint of things he was nearly ready to test. Before he realized what he was doing, Grant took her arm and swung her to face him.

There was no surprise in her face as she looked at him, but excitement—and an arousal he knew came from the sea. Her eyes mirrored it and tempted.

"I wondered last night why anyone would choose to live here." She tossed the hair from her eyes. "Now I wonder how anyone lives anywhere else." She pointed to a small fishing boat at the end of the pier. "Is that yours?"

Grant continued to stare at her, realizing abruptly he'd nearly hauled her against him and kissed her—so nearly he could all but taste her mouth against his. With an effort he turned his head in the direction she pointed. "Yes, it's mine."

"I'm keeping you from your work." For the first time, Gennie gave him the simple gift of a real smile. "I suppose you'd have been up at dawn if I hadn't gotten in the way."

With an unintelligible mutter as an answer, Grant began to propel her toward his pickup. Sighing, Gennie gave up her morning vow to be friendly as a bad bet. "Mr. Campbell, do you have to be so unpleasant?"

Grant stopped long enough to shoot her a look—one Gennie would have sworn was laced with amused irony. "Yes."

"You do it very well," she managed as he began to pull her along again.

"I've had years of practice." He released her when they reached the truck, then opened his door and got in. Without comment, Gennie skirted the hood and climbed in the passenger side.

The engine roared into life, a sound so closely associated with towns and traffic, Gennie thought it a sacrilege. She looked back once as he started down the bumpy road and knew instantly she would paint—had to paint—that scene. She nearly stated her intention out loud, then caught a glimpse of Grant's frowning profile.

The hell with him, Gennie decided. She'd paint while he was out catching lobsters or whatever he caught out there. What he didn't know wouldn't hurt her, in this case. She sat back in the seat, primly folded her hands, and kept quiet.

Grant drove a mile before he started to feel guilty. The road was hardly better than a ditch, and at night it would have been a dark series of ruts and rocks. Anyone walking over that stretch in a storm had to have been exhausted, miserable. Anyone who hadn't known the way would have been half terrified as well. He hadn't exactly dripped sympathy and concern. Still frowning, he took another quick look at her as the truck bounced along. She didn't look fragile, but he never would have believed she'd walked so far in that weather along a dark, rutted road.

He started to form what Gennie would have been astonished to hear was an apology when she lifted her chin. "There's my car." Her voice was distantly polite again—master to servant this time. Grant swallowed the apology.

He swung toward her car, jostling Gennie in her seat a bit more than was absolutely necessary. Neither of them commented as he switched off the engine and climbed out. Grant popped the hood of her car, while Gennie stood with her hands in the back pockets of her jeans.

He talked to himself, she noticed, softly, just under his breath, as he fiddled with whatever people fiddled with under hoods of cars. She supposed it was a natural enough thing for someone who lived alone at the edge of a cliff. Then again, she thought with a grin, there were times in the thickly populated *Vieux Carré* when she found herself the very best person to converse with.

Grant walked back to his truck, pulling a toolbox out of the back of the cab. He rummaged around, chose a couple of different-sized wrenches, and returned to dive under her hood again. Pursing her lips, Gennie moved behind him to peer over his shoulder. He seemed to know what he was about, she decided. And a couple of wrenches didn't seem so complicated. If she could just... She leaned in closer, automatically resting her hand on his back to keep her balance.

Grant didn't straighten, but turned, his arm brushing firmly across her breast with the movement. It could easily happen to strangers in a crowded elevator and hardly be noticed. Both of them felt the power of contact, and the surge of need.

Gennie would have backed up if she hadn't so suddenly found herself staring into those dark, restless eyes—feeling that warm, quick breath against her lips. Another inch, she thought, just another inch and it would be his mouth on hers instead of just the hint of it. Her hand had slipped to his shoulder, and without her realizing it, her fingers had tightened there.

Grant felt the pressure, but it was nothing compared to what had sprung up at the back of his neck, the base of his spine, the pit of his stomach. To take what was within his reach might relieve the pressure, or it might combust it. At the moment Grant wasn't certain what result he'd prefer.

"What are you doing?" he demanded, but this time his voice wasn't edged with anger.

Dazed, Gennie continued to stare into his eyes. She could see herself in there, she thought numbly. When did she get lost in there? "What?"

They were still leaning into the car, Gennie with her hand on his shoulder, Grant with one hand on a bolt, the other on a wrench. He had only to shift his weight to bring them together. He nearly did before he remembered how uncomfortably right she had looked standing on his land gazing out to sea.

Touch this one, Campbell, and you're in trouble, the kind of trouble a man doesn't walk away from whistling a tune.

"I asked what you were doing," he said in the same quiet tone, but his gaze slid down to her mouth.

"Doing?..." What *had* she been doing? "I-ah-I wanted to see how you fixed it so..." His gaze swept up and locked on hers again, scattered every coherent thought.

"So?" Grant repeated, enjoying the fact that he could confuse her.

"So..." His breath whispered over her lips. She caught herself running her tongue along them to taste it. "So if it happens again I could fix it."

Grant smiled—slowly, deliberately. Insolently? Gennie wasn't sure, but her heart rose to her throat and stuck there. However he smiled, whatever his intent, it added a wicked, irresistible charm to his face. She thought it was a smile a barbarian might have given his woman before he tossed her over his shoulder and took her into some dark cave. Just as slowly, he turned away to begin working with the wrench again.

Gennie backed up and let out a long, quiet breath. That had been close—too close. To what, she wasn't precisely sure, but to something no smart woman would consider safe. She cleared her throat. "Do you think you can fix it?"

"Hmmm."

Gennie took this for the affirmative, then stepped closer, this time keeping to the side of the hood. "A mechanic looked at it a couple weeks ago."

"Think you're going to need new plugs soon. I'd have Buck Gates take a look if I were you."

"Is he a mechanic? At the service station?"

Grant straightened. He wasn't smiling now, but there was amusement in his eyes. "There's no service station in Windy Point. You need gas, you go down to the docks and pump it. You got car trouble, you see Buck Gates. He repairs the lobster boats—a motor's a motor." The last was delivered in an easy Down East cadence, with a hint of a smile that had nothing to do with condescension. "Start her up."

Leaving her door open, Gennie slid behind the wheel. A turn of the key had her engine springing cheerfully to life. Even as she let out a relieved sigh, Grant slammed the hood into place. Gennie cut the engine again as he walked back to his truck to replace his tools.

"The Lawrence cottage's about three quarters of a mile up on the left. You can't miss the turnoff unless you're hiking through a storm in the middle of the night with only a flashlight."

Gennie swallowed a chuckle. Don't let him have any redeeming qualities, she pleaded. Let me remember him as a rude, nasty man who just happens to be fatally sexy. "I'll keep that in mind."

"And I wouldn't mention that you'd spent the night at Windy Point Station," he added easily as he slipped the toolbox back into place. "I have a reputation to protect."

This time she bit her lip to hold back a smile. "Oh?"

"Yeah." Grant turned back, leaning against the truck a moment as he looked at her again. "The villagers think I'm odd. I'd slip a couple notches if they found out I hadn't just shoved you back outside and locked the door."

This time she did smile—but only a little. "You have my word, no one will hear from me what a good samaritan you are. If anyone should happen to ask, I'll tell them you're rude, disagreeable, and generally nasty."

"I'd appreciate it."

When he started to climb back into the truck, Gennie reached for her wallet. "Wait, I haven't paid you for—"

"Forget it."

She hooked her hand on the door handle. "I don't want to be obligated to you for—"

"Tough." Grant started the engine. "Look, move your car, I can't turn around with you in my way."

Eyes narrowed, she whirled away. So much for gratitude, she told herself. So the villagers thought he was odd, she mused as she slammed the car door. Perceptive people. Gennie started down the road at a cautious speed, making it a point not to look into the rearview mirror. When she came to the turnoff, she veered left. The only sign of Grant Campbell was the steady hum of his truck as he went on. Gennie told herself she wouldn't think of him again.

And she didn't as she drove down the straight little lane with black-eyed Susans springing up on either side. The sound of his truck was a distant echo, soon lost. Without any trees to block the view, Gennie saw the cottage almost immediately, and was charmed. Small certainly, but it didn't evoke images of seven dwarfs heigh-hoing. Gennie immediately had a picture of a tidy woman in a housedress hanging out the wash, then a rough-featured fisherman whittling on the tiny porch.

It had been painted blue but had weathered to a soft blue-gray. A one-story boxlike structure, it had a modest front porch facing the lane and, she was to discover, another screened porch looking out over the inlet. A pier that looked like it might be a bit shaky stretched out over the glassily calm water. Someone had planted a willow near the shore, but it wasn't flourishing.

Gennie turned off the engine and was struck with silence. Pleasant, peaceful—yes, she could live with this, work with this. Yet she discovered she preferred the thrash and boom of the sea that Grant had outside his front door.

Oh, no, she reminded herself firmly, she vowed not to think of him. And she wouldn't. After stepping from the car, Gennie hefted the first box of groceries and climbed the plank stairs to the front door. She had to fight with the lock a moment, then it gave a mighty groan and yielded.

The first thing Gennie noticed was tidiness. The Widow Lawrence had meant what she said when she had stated the cottage was clean. The furniture was draped in dustcovers but there was no dust. Obviously, she came in regularly and chased it away. Gennie found the idea touching and sad. The walls were painted a pale blue, and the lighter patches here and there indicated where pictures had hung for years. Carrying her box of supplies, Gennie wandered toward the back of the house and found the kitchen.

The sense of order prevailed here as well. Formica counters were spotless, the porcelain sink gleamed. A flick of the tap proved the plumbing was indeed cooperative. Gennie set down the box and went through the back door onto the screened porch. The air was warm and moist, tasting of the sea. Someone had repaired a few holes in the screen and the paint on the floor was cracked but clean.

Too clean, Gennie realized. There was no sign of life in the cottage, and barely any echo of the life that had once been there. She would have preferred the dusty disorder she had found in Grant's lighthouse. Someone *lived* there. Someone vital. Shaking her head, she pushed him to the back of her mind. Someone lived here now—and in short order the house would know it. Quickly she went back to her car to unpack.

Because she traveled light and was inherently organized, it took less than two hours for Gennie to distribute her things throughout the house. Both bedrooms were tiny, and only one had a bed. When Gennie made it up with the linens she had bought, she discovered it was a feather bed. Delighted, she spent some time bouncing on it and sinking into it. In the second bedroom she stowed her painting gear. With the dustcovers removed and a few of her own paintings hung on the faded spots, she began to feel a sense of home.

Barefoot and pleased with herself, she went out to walk the length of the pier. A few boards creaked and others shook, but she decided the structure was safe enough. Perhaps she would buy a small boat and explore the inlet. She could do as she pleased now, go where she liked. Her ties in New Orleans would pull her back eventually, but the wanderlust which had driven her north six months before had yet to fade.

Wanderlust, she repeated as her eyes clouded. No, the word was guilt—or pain. It was still following her, perhaps it always would. It's been more than a year, Gennie thought as she closed her eyes. Seventeen months, two weeks, three days. And she could still see Angela. Perhaps she should be grateful for that—for the fact that her artist's memory could conjure up her sister's face exactly as it had been. Young, beautiful, vibrant. But on the other side of the coin, it was too easy to see Angela lifeless and broken—the way her sister had looked after she'd killed her.

Not your fault. How many times had she heard that?

It wasn't your fault, Gennie. You can't blame yourself.

Oh, yes, I can, she thought with a sigh. If I hadn't been driving... If my reflexes had been quicker... If I'd only seen that car running the red light.

There was no going back, and Gennie knew it. The times the helpless guilt and grief flooded her were fewer now, but no less painful. She had her art, and sometimes she thought that alone had saved her sanity after her sister's death. All in all this trip had been good for her—by taking her away from the memories that were still too close, and by letting her concentrate on painting for painting's sake.

Art had become too much like a business to her in the past few years. She'd nearly lost herself in the selling and showings. Now it was back to basics—she needed that. Oil, acrylic, watercolor, charcoal; and the canvases that waited to be filled.

Perhaps the hard realism of losing her sister had influenced her to seek the same hard realism in her work. It might have been her way of forcing herself to accept life, and death. Her abstracts, the misty quality of her painting had always given the world she created a gentle hue. Not quite real but so easy to believe in. Now she was drawn to the plain, the everyday. Reality wasn't always pretty, but there was a strength in it she was just beginning to understand.

Gennie drew in a deep breath. Yes, she would paint this—this quiet, settled little inlet. There'd be a time for it. But first, now, she needed the challenge and power of the ocean. A glance at her watch showed her it was noon. Surely he would be out on his boat now, making up the time she had cost him that morning. She could have three or four hours to sketch the lighthouse from different angles without him even knowing. And if he did, Gennie added with a shrug, what difference would it make? One woman with a sketch pad could hardly bother him. In any case, he could just bolt himself up inside and ignore her if he didn't like it. Just as she intended to ignore him.

Grant's studio was on the third level. More precisely, Grant's studio *was* the third level. What had been three cubbyhole rooms had been remodeled into one with good natural light, strongest from the north. Glass-topped cabinets, called taborets, held an assortment of tools, completely organized. Fountain pens, ballpoints, knives, sable brushes, a wide variety of pencils and erasers, bow compass, T square. An engineer or architect would have recognized several of the tools and approved the quality. Matte paper was already taped down to his drawing board.

On the whitewashed wall he faced hung a mirror and a framed reprint of *The Yellow Kid*, a cartoon strip nearly a hundred years old. On the other side of the room was a sophisticated radio and a small color TV. The stack of newspapers and magazines in the corner was waist-high. The room had the sense of practical order Grant bothered with in no other aspect of his life.

He worked without hurry this morning. There were times he worked frantically, not because of a deadline—he was always a month ahead of schedule—but because his own thoughts pushed at him. At times he would take a week or perhaps two to simply gather ideas and store them. Other times, he would work through the night as those same ideas fretted to be put down with pen and ink.

He'd finished the project he'd been working on in the early hours of the morning. Now a new angle had been pushing at him, one he didn't seem to be able to resist. Grant rarely resisted anything that applied to his art. Already he had scaled the paper, striking diagonal lines with the blue pencil that wouldn't photograph. He knew what he wanted, but the preparation came first, those finite, vital details no one would ever notice in the few seconds it took to view his work.

When the paper was set and scaled, divided into five sections double the size they would be when reproduced, he began to sketch lightly. Doodling really, he brought his main character to life with a few loops and lines. The man was quite ordinary. Grant had insisted he be when he had created what his sister called his alter ego ten years before. An ordinary man, perhaps a bit scruffy, with a few features—the nose, the puzzled eyes—a bit exaggerated. But Grant's Macintosh was easily recognizable as someone you might pass on the street. And barely notice.

He was always too thin so that his attempts at dressing sharply never quite came off. He carried the air of someone who knew he was going to be put upon. Grant had a certain fondness for his general ineptitude and occasional satirical remarks.

Grant knew all of his friends—he'd created them as well. Not precisely a motley crew, but very close. Well-meaning dreamers, smart alecks. They were the shades of the people Grant had known in college—friends and acquaintances. Ordinary people doing ordinary things in an unusual way. That was the theme of his craft.

He'd given birth to Macintosh in college, then had left him in a closet while he had pursued art in a more traditional manner for almost three years. Perhaps he would have been successful; the talent had been there.

But Grant had discovered he was much happier sketching a caricature than painting a portrait. In the end Macintosh had won. Grant had hauled him back out of the closet, and at the end of seven years the slightly weary, bleary-eyed character appeared in every major newspaper in the country seven days a week.

People followed his life and times over coffee, on the subway, on buses, and in bed. Over a million Americans opened their newspapers and looked to see just what he was up to that day before they had to face their own.

As a cartoonist, Grant knew it was his responsibility to amuse, and to amuse quickly, with a few short sentences and simple drawings. The strip would be looked at for ten or twelve seconds, chuckled over, then tossed aside. Often to line a bird cage. Grant had few illusions. It was the chuckle that was important, the fact that for those few seconds, he had given people something to laugh at—something to relate to. In *Macintosh*, Grant looked for the common experience, then twisted it.

What he wanted, what he insisted on having, was the right to do so, and the right to be left alone to do it. He was known to the public only by his initials. His contract with United Syndicate specifically stated his name would never be used in conjunction with the strip, nor would he grant any interviews or do any guest spots. His anonymity was as much a part of his price as his annual income.

Still using only the pencil, he began on the second section—Macintosh mumbling as the thudding on the door interrupted his newest hobby. Stamp collecting. Grant had gotten two full weeks out of this particular angle—Macintosh's bumbling attempts, his friends' caustic comments about his terminal boredom. Macintosh had fussed with his stamps and wondered if he'd finally hit a gold mine as the television had droned on behind him on the latest increase in the first-class mail service.

Here, he would open his door to be faced with a wet, bad-tempered siren. Grant didn't have any trouble drawing Gennie. In fact, he felt making her a character would put her firmly in perspective. She'd be just as ridiculous, and as vulnerable, as the rest of the people in his world. He'd begin to think of her as a character instead of a woman—flesh, blood, soft, fragrant. He didn't have any room for a woman, but he always had room for a character. He could tell them when to come, when to go, what to say.

He named her Veronica, thinking the more sophisticated name suited her. Deliberately, he exaggerated the tilt of her eyes and the lush sensuality of her mouth. Since the setting was Washington, D.C., rather than coastal Maine, Grant gave her a flat tire on the way home from a White House function. Macintosh goggled at her. Grant captured this by giving himself several stunned stares in the mirror above the drawing board.

He worked for two hours, perfecting the storyline—the situation, the setup, the punchline. After changing her tire and practicing macho lines to impress her, Macintosh ended up with five dollars, a stutter, and soaked shoes as Veronica zoomed out of his life.

Grant felt better when the sketches were done. He'd put Gennie just where he wanted—driving away. Now he would detail his work with India ink and brush. Solid black would accent or focus, the Benday patterns—zones of dots or lines—would give the gray areas.

Detailing Macintosh's room was simple enough; Grant had been there a thousand times. But it still took time and precision. Balance was crucial, the angles and positioning in order to draw the reader's attention just where you wanted it for the few seconds they would look at the individual panel. His supply of patience was consumed by his work, giving him little for the other areas of his life. The strip was half finished and the afternoon waning before he stopped to rest his hand.

Coffee, he thought, stretching his back and shoulders as he noticed the ache. And food. Breakfast had been too long ago. He'd grab something and take a walk down on the beach. He still had two papers to read and a few hours of television. Too much could happen in a day for him to ignore either form of communication. But the walk came first, Grant decided as he moved idly to the window. He needed some fresh air...

The hand he had lifted to rub at the back of his neck dropped. Leaning closer, he narrowed his eyes and stared down. It was bad enough when he had to deal with the occasional stray tourist, he thought furiously. A few curt words sent them away and kept them away. But there was no mistaking, even at this height, that thick ebony hair.

Veronica had yet to drive out of his life.

Chapter Three

It was beautiful, no matter what angle you chose or how the light shifted. Gennie had a half dozen sketches in her pad and knew she could have a half dozen more without catching all the aspects of that one particular jut of land. Look at the colors in the rocks! Would she ever be able to capture them? And the way the lighthouse stood there, solid, indomitable. The whitewash was faded here and there, the concrete blocks pockmarked with time and salt spray. That only added to the humanity of it. Man's strike for safety against the mercurial sea.

There would have been times the sea would have won, Gennie mused. Because man was fallible. There would have been times the lighthouse would have won. Because man was tenacious. Pitted together they spoke of harmony, perseverance, sweat, and strength.

She lost track of the time she had sat there, undisturbed, disturbing no one. Yet she knew she could go on sitting as long as the sun gave enough light. There were so few places in New Orleans where she could go to paint without the distractions of curiosity seekers or art buffs. When she chose to paint in the city, she was invariably recognized, and once recognized, watched or questioned.

Even when she went out—into the bayou, along a country road, she was often followed. She'd grown used to working around that and to saving most of her serious work for her studio. Over the years she'd nearly forgotten the simple freedom of being able to work outdoors, having the advantage of smelling and tasting what you drew while you drew it.

The past six months had given her something she hadn't been aware she'd looked for—a reminder of what she had been before success had put its limitations on her.

Content, half dreaming, she sketched what she saw and felt, and needed nothing else.

"Damn it, what do you want now?"

To her credit, Gennie didn't jolt or drop her sketch pad. She'd known Grant was around somewhere as his boat hadn't been moved. And she'd already decided he wasn't going to spoil what she'd found here. She was arrogant enough to feel it her right to be there to paint what her art demanded she paint. Thinking he was rather casual about his trade as a fisherman, she turned to him.

He was furious, she thought mildly. But she'd hardly seen him any other way. She decided he was suited to the out-of-doors—the sun, the wind, and the sea. Perhaps she'd do a sketch or two of him before she was finished. Tilting her head back, Gennie studied him as she would any subject that interested her.

"Good afternoon," she said in her best plantation drawl.

Knowing he was being measured and insulted might have amused him under different circumstances. At the moment it made him yearn to give her a hefty shove off her rock. All he wanted was for her to go away, and stay away—before he gave in to the urge to touch her.

"I asked you what you wanted."

"No need for you to bother. I'm just taking some preliminary sketches." Gennie kept her seat on the contorted rock near the verge of the cliff and shifted back to sea. "You can just go on with whatever you were doing."

Grant's eyes narrowed to dark slits. Oh, she was good at this, he thought. Dismissing underlings. "You're on my land."

"Mmm-hmm."

The idea of helping her off the rock became more appealing. "You're trespassing."

Gennie sent him an indulgent glance over her left shoulder. "You should try barbed wire and land mines. Nothing like a land mine to make a statement. Not that I can blame you for wanting to keep this little slice of the world to yourself, Grant," she added as she began to sketch again. "But I'm going to leave it exactly as I found it—no pop cans, no paper plates, no cigarette butts."

Even lifted over the roar of the sea, her voice held a mild, deliberately placating tone designed to set nerve ends on edge. Grant came very close to grabbing her by the hair and dragging her to her feet when he was distracted by her pencil moving over the paper. What he saw halted the oath on the tip of his tongue.

It was more than good, too true to life for a mere excellent. With dashes and shading, she was capturing the swirl of the sea on rock, the low swoop of gulls and the steady endurance of the lighthouse. In the same way, she'd given the sketch no hint of quiet beauty. It was all hard edges, chips, flaws, and simplicity. It wouldn't make a postcard, nor would it make a soothing touch of art over a mantel. But anyone who'd ever stood on a point where sea battled shore would understand it.

Frowning in concentration rather than anger, Grant bent closer. Hers weren't the hands of a student; hers wasn't the soul of an amateur. In silence Grant waited until she had finished, then immediately took the sketchbook from her.

"Hey!" Gennie was halfway off her rock.

"Shut up."

She did, only because she saw he wasn't going to hurl her work into the sea. Settling back on her rock, she watched Grant as he flipped through her pages. Now and again he stopped to study one sketch a bit longer than the others.

His eyes were very dark now, she noted, while the wind blew his hair over his forehead and away again. There was a line, not of temper but of intensity, between his brows. His mouth was unsmiling, set, Gennie thought, to judge. It should have amused her to have her work critiqued by a reclusive fisherman. Somehow it didn't. There was a faint ache behind her temple she recognized as tension. She'd felt that often enough before every one of her showings.

Grant's eyes skimmed over the page and met hers. For a long moment there was only the crash of the surf and the distant bell of a buoy. Now he knew why he'd had that nagging sense of having seen her before. But her newspaper pictures didn't do her justice. "Grandeau," he said at length. "Geneviève Grandeau."

At any other time she wouldn't have been surprised to have had her work or her name recognized. Not in New York, California, Atlanta. But it was intriguing to find a man at some forgotten land's end who could recognize her work from a rough sketch in a notepad.

"Yes." She stood then, combing her hair back from her forehead with her hand and holding it there. "How did you know?"

He tapped the sketchbook on his palm while his eyes stayed on hers. "Technique is technique whether it's sketches or oils. What's the toast of New Orleans doing in Windy Point?"

The dry tone of the question annoyed her enough that she forgot how easily he had recognized her work. "I'm taking a year's sabbatical." Rising, she held out her hand for her pad.

Grant ignored the gesture. "An odd place to find one of the country's most...social artists. Your work's in art papers almost as often as your name's in the society section. Weren't you engaged to an Italian count last year?"

"He was a baron," she corrected coolly, "and we weren't engaged. Do you fill your time between catches reading the tabloids?"

The flash of temper in her eyes made him grin. "I do quite a bit of reading. And you," he added before she could think of some retort, "manage to get yourself in the *New York Times* almost as often as you get yourself in the tabloids and the glossies."

Gennie tossed her head in a gesture so reminiscent of royal displeasure, his grin widened. "It seems some live and others only read about life."

"You do make good copy, Genvième." He couldn't resist, and hooked his thumbs in his pockets as new ideas for Veronica raced through his mind. It seemed inevitable that she would come back and drive Macintosh crazy for a while. "You're a favorite with the paparazzi."

Her voice remained cool and distant, but she began to tap her pencil against the rock. "I suppose they have to make their living like anyone else."

"I seem to recall something about a duel being fought in Brittany a couple of years ago."

A smile lit her face, full of fun, when he hadn't expected it. "If you believe that, I have a bridge in New York you might be interested in."

"Don't spoil my illusions," Grant said mildly. The smile wasn't easy to resist, he discovered, not when it was genuine and touched with self-deprecating humor.

"If you'd rather believe tripe," she said graciously, "who am I to argue?"

Better to keep digging at her than to dwell too long on that smile. "Some tripe's fascinating in its way. There was a film director before the count—"

"Baron," Gennie reminded him. "The count you're thinking of was French, and one of my first patrons."

"You've had quite a selection of...patrons."

She continued to smile, obviously amused. "Yes. Are you an art buff or do you just like gossip?"

"Both," he told her easily. "Come to think of it, there hasn't been a great deal about your—adventures—in the press for the last few months. You're obviously keeping your sabbatical very low key. The last thing I recall reading was..."

He remembered then and could have cut out his tongue. The car accident—her sister's death—a beautiful and intrusive wire-service photo of Geneviève Grandeau at the funeral. Devastation, shock, grief; that much had been clear even through the veil she had worn.

She wasn't smiling now, but looking at him with a mask of placid blankness. "I'm sorry," he said.

The apology nearly buckled her knees. She'd heard those words so many times before, from so many different people, but they'd never struck her with such simple sincerity. From a stranger, Gennie thought as she turned toward the sea again. It shouldn't mean so much coming from a stranger.

"It's all right." The wind felt so cool, so vital. It wasn't the place to dwell on death. If she had to think of it, she would think of it when she was alone, when there was silence. Now she could breathe deep and drink in the sea, and the strength. "So you spend your leisure time reading all the gossip in this wicked world. For a man who's so interested in people, you chose a strange place to live."

"Interested in them," Grant agreed, grateful that she was stronger than she looked. "That doesn't mean I want to be around them."

"You don't care for people, then." When she turned back, the smile was there again, teasing. "The tough recluse. In a few years you might even make crusty."

"You can't be crusty until you're fifty," he countered. "It's an unwritten law."

"I don't know." Gennie stuck her pencil behind her ear and tilted her head. "I wouldn't think you'd bother with laws, unwritten or otherwise."

"Depends," he said simply, "on whether they're useful or not."

She laughed. "Tell me..." She glanced down to the sketchbook Grant still held. "Do you like the sketches?"

He gave a short laugh. "I don't think Genviève Grandeau needs an unsolicited critique."

"Genviève has a tremendous ego," Gennie corrected. "Besides, it's not unsolicited if I ask for it."

Grant gave her a long, steady look before answering. "Your work's always very moving, very personal. The publicity attached to it isn't necessary."

"I believe, from you, that's a compliment," Gennie considered. "Are you going to give me free rein to paint here, or am I going to have to fight you every step of the way?"

He frowned again, and his face settled into the lines so quickly, Gennie swallowed a laugh. "Why here, precisely?"

"I was beginning to think you were perceptive," Gennie said with a sigh. She made a sweep with her hand, wide, graceful, encompassing. "Can't you see it? It's life and it's death. It's a war that never ends, one we'll never see the outcome of. I can put that on canvas—only a part of it, a small, small slice. But I can do it. I couldn't resist if I wanted to."

"The last thing I want here is a bunch of eager reporters or a few displaced European noblemen."

Gennie lifted a brow, at once haughty and amused. It was the casual superiority of the look, Grant told himself, that made him want to drag her to the ground and prove to them both she was only a woman. "I think you take your reading too seriously," she told him in an infuriatingly soft drawl. "But I could give my word, if you like, that I won't phone the press or any of the two dozen lovers you seem to think I have."

"Don't you?" His banked temper came out in sarcasm. Gennie met it coolly.

"That's none of your business. However," she continued, "I could sign a contract in blood—yours preferably—and pay you a reasonable fee, since it's your lighthouse. I'm going to paint here, with your cooperation or without it."

"You seem to have a disregard for property rights, Genviève."

"You seem to have a disregard for the rights of art."

He laughed at that, a sound that was appealing, masculine, and puzzling. "No," he said after a moment, "as it happens, I feel very strongly about the rights of the artist."

"As long as it doesn't involve you."

He sighed, a sound she recognized as frustrated. His feelings about art and censorship were too ingrained to allow him to bar her way. And he knew, even as he stood there, that she was going to give him a great deal of trouble. A pity she hadn't chosen Penobscot Bay. "Paint," he said briefly. "And stay out of my way."

"Agreed." Gennie stepped up on the rock and looked out to sea again. "It's your rocks I want, your house, your sea." The lazily feminine smile touched her lips as she turned to him again. "But you're quite safe, Grant. I haven't any designs on you."

It was bait, they both knew it. But he nibbled anyway. "You don't worry me, Genviève."

"Don't I?" *What are you doing?* her common sense demanded. She ignored it. He thought she was some kind of twentieth-century siren. Why not humor him? With the aid of the rock she was a few inches above him. His eyes were narrowed against the sun as he looked up at her, hers were wide and smiling. With a laugh, she rested her hands on his shoulders. "I could have sworn I did."

Grant considered simply yanking her from the rock and into his arms. He ignored the stab of desire that came so quickly then left a nagging ache. She was taunting him, damn her, and she would win if he wasn't careful. "It's your ego again," he told her. "You're not the type that appeals to me."

Anger flashed into her eyes again, making her nearly irresistible. "Does any?"

"I prefer a softer type," he said, knowing her skin would be soft enough to melt if he gave in and put his hands on her. "Quieter," he lied. "Someone a bit less aggressive."

Gennie struggled not to lose her temper completely and slug him. "Ah, you prefer women who sit silently and don't think."

"Who don't flaunt their—attributes." This time his smile was taunting. "I don't have any trouble resisting you."

The bait was cast again, and this time Gennie swallowed it whole. "Really? Let's see about that."

She brought her mouth down to his before she had a chance to consider the consequences. Her hands were still on his shoulders, his still in his pockets, but the contact of lips brought on a full-scale explosion. Grant felt it rocket through him, fierce and fast, while his fingers balled into fists.

What in God's name was this? he demanded while he used every ounce of control not to bring her body against his. Instinctively he knew that would be the end for him. He had only to weather this one assault on his system, and it would be over.

Why didn't he back away? He wasn't chained. Grant told himself to, ordered himself to, then stood helpless while her mouth moved over his. Dozens, dozens of images and fantasies rained in his head until he nearly drowned in them. Witch, he thought as his mind hazed. He'd been right about her all along. He felt the ground tilt under his feet, the roar of the sea fill his brain. Her taste, warm, mysterious, spiced with woman, seeped into everything. And even that wasn't enough. For a moment he believed that there could be more than everything, a step just beyond what men knew. Perhaps women understood it. He felt his body tense as though he'd been shot. Perhaps this woman did.

In some part of his brain, he knew that for one brief moment he was completely vulnerable.

Gennie drew away quickly. Grant thought he felt the hands still on his shoulders tremble lightly. Her eyes were dazed, her lips parted not in temptation but in astonishment. Through his own shock, he realized she'd been just as moved as he, and just as weakened by it.

"I-I have to go," she began, then bit her lip as she realized she was stuttering again—a habit she seemed to have developed in the past twenty-four hours. Forgetting her sketch pad, she stepped off the rock and prepared to make an undignified dash for her car. In the next instant she was whirled around.

His face was set, his breathing unsteady. "I was wrong." His voice filled her head, emptying it of everything else. "I have a great deal of trouble resisting you."

What had she done, Gennie wondered frantically, to both of them? She was trembling—she never trembled. Frightened? Oh, God, yes. She could face the storm and the dark now with complete confidence. It was nothing compared to this. "I think we'd better—"

"So do I," he muttered as he hauled her against him. "But it's too late now."

In the next instant his mouth covered hers, hard, undeniable. But she would deny it, Gennie told herself. She had to or be swallowed up. How had she ever thought she understood emotions, sensations? Translating them with paints was nothing compared with an onslaught of experience. He poured through her until she wasn't certain she'd ever be free of him.

She lifted her hands to push him away. She drew him yet closer. His fingers gripped her hair, not gently. The savageness of the cliff, the sea, the wind, tore into both of them and ruled. He tugged her head back, perhaps to pretend he was still in command. Her lips parted, and her tongue raced to meet his.

Is this what she'd always ached to feel? Gennie wondered. This wild liberation, this burning, searing need? She'd never known what it was like to be so filled with another's taste that you could remember no others. She'd known he had this kind of strength in him, had sensed it from the first. But to feel it now, to know she was caught up in it was such a conflicting emotion—power and weakness—that she couldn't tell one from the other.

His skin was rough, scraping against hers as he slanted his mouth to a new angle. Feeling the small, intimate pain, she moaned from the sheer pleasure of it. His hands were still in her hair, roaming, gripping, tangling, while their mouths met in mutual assault.

Let yourself go. It was an order that came from somewhere deep inside of her. Let yourself feel. Helpless, she obeyed.

She heard the gulls, but the sound seemed romantic now, no longer mournful. The sea beat against the land. Power, power, power. She knew the full extent of it as her lips clung to Grant's. The edge of the cliff was close, she knew. One step, two, and she would be over, cartwheeling into space to be brought up short by the hard earth of reality. But those few seconds of giddy freedom would be worth the risk. Her sigh spoke of yielding and of triumph.

Grant swore, the sound muffled against her lips before he could force himself to break away from her. This was exactly what he had sworn wouldn't happen. He'd done enough fishing to know when he was being reeled in. He didn't have time for this—that's what he told himself as he looked down at Gennie. Her face was soft, flushed with passion, her hair trailing down to be tugged at by the wind as she kept her head tilted back. His lips ached to press against that slender, golden throat. It was her eyes, half closed and gleaming with the ageless power of woman, that helped him resist. It was a trap he wouldn't be caught in no matter which of them baited it.

His voice was low when he spoke, and as furious as his eyes. "I might want you. I might even take you. But it'll be when I'm damn good and ready. You want to call the tune, play the games, stick with your counts and your barons." Grant whirled away, cursing both of them.

Too stunned to move, Gennie watched him disappear inside the lighthouse. Was that all it had meant to him? she thought numbly. Just any man, any woman, any passion? Hadn't he felt that quicksilver pain that had meant unity, intimacy, destiny? Games? How could he talk of games after they had... Closing her eyes, she ran an unsteady hand through her hair.

No, it was her fault. She was making something out of nothing. There was no unity between two people who didn't even know each other, and intimacy was just a handy word to justify the needs of the physical. She was being fanciful again, turning something ordinary into something special because it was what she wanted.

Let him go. She reached down to pick up her sketch pad and found the pencil Grant had dislodged from her hair. Let him go, and concentrate on your work, she ordered herself. It was the scene that carried you away, not the content. Careful not to look back, she walked to her car.

Her hands didn't stop trembling until she reached the lane to the cottage. This was better, she thought as she listened to the quiet lap of water and the gentle sounds of swallows coming back to nest for the evening. There was peace here, and the light was easy. This was what she should paint instead of the turbulence of the ocean and the ruggedness of rocks. This was where she should stay, soaking up the drifting solitude of still water and calm air. When you challenged the tempestuousness of nature, odds were you lost. Only a fool continued to press against the odds.

Suddenly weary, Gennie got out of the car and wandered down to the pier. At the end she sat down on the rough wood to let her feet dangle over the side. If she stayed here, she'd be safe.

She sat in silence while the sun lowered in the sky. It took no effort to feel the lingering pressure of Grant's lips on hers. She'd never known a man to kiss like that—forceful, consuming, yet with a trace of vulnerability. Then again, she wasn't as experienced as Grant assumed.

She dated, she socialized, she enjoyed men's company, but as her art had always come first, her more intimate relationships were limited. Classes, work, showings, traveling, parties: almost everything she'd ever done for almost as long as she could remember had been connected with her art, and the need to express it.

Certainly she enjoyed the social benefits, the touches of glitter and glamor that came her way after days and weeks of isolation. She didn't mind the image the press had created, because it seemed rather unique and bohemian. She didn't mind taking a bit of glitz here and there after working herself to near exhaustion in silence and solitude. At times the Genviève the papers tattled about amused or impressed her. Then it would be time for the next painting. She'd never had any trouble tucking the socialite away from the artist.

Wouldn't the press be shocked, Gennie mused, to learn that Genviève Grandeau of the New Orleans Grandeaus, successful artist, established socialite, and woman of the world had never had a lover?

With a half laugh, she leaned back on her elbows. She'd been wedded to her art for so long, a lover had seemed superfluous. Until... Gennie started to block out the thought, then calling herself a coward, finished it out. Until Grant Campbell.

Staring up at the sky, she let herself remember those sensations, those feelings and needs he'd unlocked in her. She would have made love with him without a thought, without a moment's hesitation. He'd rejected her.

No, it was more than that, Gennie remembered as anger began to rise again. Rejection was one thing, painful, humiliating, but that hadn't been all of it. Grant had dumped his arrogance on top of rejection—that was intolerable.

He'd said he'd *take* her when *he* was ready. As if she were a-a chocolate bar on a store counter. Her eyes narrowed, pale green with fury. We'll see about that, Gennie told herself. We'll just see about that!

Standing, she brushed off the seat of her pants with one clean swipe. No one rejected Genviève Grandeau. And no one took her. It was games he wanted, she thought as she stalked toward the cottage, it would be games he'd get.

Chapter Four

She wasn't going to be chased away. Gennie told herself that with a grim satisfaction as she packed her painting gear the next morning. *No one* chased her away—especially a rude, arrogant idiot. Grant Campbell was going to find her perched on his doorstep—in a manner of speaking—until she was good and ready to move on.

The painting, Gennie mused as she checked her brushes. Of course the painting was of first importance, but...while she was about it, she thought with a tight smile, she would take a bit of time to teach that man a lesson. Oh, he deserved one. Gennie tossed the hair out of her eyes as she shut the lid on her paint box. No one, in all of her experience, deserved a good dig in the ribs as much as Grant Campbell. And she was just the woman to give it to him.

So he thought she wanted to play games. Gennie snapped the locks on the case a bit violently, so that the sound echoed like two shots through the empty cottage. She'd play games all right—her games, her rules.

Gennie had spent twenty-six years watching her grandmother beguile and enchant the male species. An amazing woman, Gennie thought now with an affectionate smile. Beautiful and vibrant in her seventies, she could still twist a man of any age around her finger. Well, she was a Genviève, too. She stuck her hands on her hips. And Grant Campbell was about to take a short walk off a high cliff.

Take me, will he? she thought, seething all over again with the memory. Of all the impossible gall. When *he's* ready? Making a low sound in her throat, she grabbed a paint smock. She'd have Grant Campbell crawling at her feet before she was through with him!

The anger and indignation Gennie had nursed all night made it easy to forget that sharp, sweet surge of response she'd felt when his mouth had been on hers. It made it easy to forget the fact that she'd wanted him—blindly, urgently—as she'd never wanted any man before. Temper was much more satisfying than depression, and Gennie rolled with it. She'd take her revenge coolly; it would taste better that way.

Satisfied that her gear was in order, Gennie walked through the cottage to her bedroom. Critically, she studied herself in the mirror over the old bureau. She was artist enough to recognize good bone structure and coloring. Perhaps suppressed anger suited her, she considered, as it added a faint rose flush to the honey tone of her skin.

As grimly as a warrior preparing for battle, she picked up a pot of muted green eyeshadow. When you had an unusual feature, she thought as she smudged it on her lids, you played it up. The result pleased her—a bit exotic, but not obvious. Lightly, she touched her lips with color—not too much, she reflected, just enough to tempt. With a lazy smile, she dabbed her scent behind her ears. Oh, she intended to tempt him all right. And when he was on his knees, she'd stroll blithely away.

A pity she couldn't wear something a bit sexier, she thought as she pursed her lips and turned sideways in the mirror. But the painting did come first, after all. One couldn't wear something slinky to sit on a rock. The jeans and narrow little top would have to do. Pleased with the day's prospects, Gennie started back for her gear when the sound of an approaching car distracted her.

Her first thought was Grant, her first reaction a flood of nerves. Annoyed, Gennie told herself it was simply the anticipation of the contest that had her heart pounding. When she went to the window, she saw it wasn't Grant's pickup, but a small, battered station wagon. The Widow Lawrence stepped out, neat and prim, carrying a covered plate. Surprised, and a bit uncomfortable, Gennie opened the door to her landlady.

"Good morning." She smiled, trying to ignore the oddness of inviting the woman inside a cottage where she had lived, slept, and worked for years.

"See you're up and about." The widow hovered at the threshold with her tiny, dark eyes on Gennie's face.

"Yes." Gennie would have taken her hand instinctively if the widow hadn't been gripping the plate with both of them. "Please, come in, Mrs. Lawrence."

"Don't want to bother you. Thought maybe you'd like some muffins."

"I would." Gennie forgot her plans for an early start and opened the door wider. "Especially if you'd have some coffee with me."

"Wouldn't mind." The widow hesitated almost imperceptibly, then stepped inside. "Can't stay long, I'm needed at the post office." But her gaze skimmed over the room as she stood in front of the door.

"They smell wonderful." Gennie took the plate and headed back toward the kitchen, hoping to dispel some of the awkwardness. "You know, I can never drum up much energy for cooking when it's only for me."

"Ayah. There's more pleasure when you've a family to feed."

Gennie felt another well of sympathy, but didn't offer it. She faced the stove as she measured out coffee in the little pot she'd bought in town. The widow would be looking at her kitchen, Gennie thought, and remembering.

"You settled in all right, then."

"Yes." Gennie took two plates and set them on the narrow drop-leaf table. "The cottage is just what I needed. It's beautiful, Mrs. Lawrence." She hesitated as she took down cups and saucers, then turned to face the woman again. "You must have hated to leave here."

Mrs. Lawrence shifted her shoulders in what might have been a shrug. "Things change. Roof hold up all right in the storm the other night?"

Gennie gave her a blank look, but caught herself before she said she hadn't been there to notice. "I didn't have any trouble," she said instead. Gennie saw the gaze wander around the room. Perhaps it would be best if she talked about it. Everyone had told Gennie that about Angela, but she hadn't believed them then. Now she began to wonder if it would help to talk about a loss instead of submerging it.

"Did you live here long, Mrs. Lawrence?" She brought the cups to the table as she asked, then went for the cream.

"Twenty-six years," the woman said after a moment. "Moved in after my second boy was born. A doctor he is, a resident in Bangor." Stiff New England pride showed in the jut of her chin. "His brother's got himself a job on an oil rig—couldn't keep away from the sea."

Gennie came to join her at the table. "You must be very proud of them."

"Ayah."

"Was your husband a fisherman?"

"Lobsterman." She didn't smile, but Gennie heard it in her voice. "A good one. Died on his boat. Stroke they tell me." She added a dab of cream to her coffee, hardly enough to change the color. "He'd've wanted to die on his boat."

She wanted to ask how long ago, but couldn't. Perhaps the time would come when she would be able to speak of the loss of her sister in such simple terms of acceptance. "Do you like living in town?"

"Used to it now. There be friends there, and this road..." For the first time, Gennie saw the wisp of a smile that made the hard, lined face almost pretty.

"My Matthew could curse this road six ways to Sunday."

"I believe it." Tempted by the aroma, Gennie removed the checkered dishcloth from the plate. "Blueberry!" She grinned, pleased. "I saw wild blueberry bushes along the road from town."

"Ayah, they'll be around a little while more." She watched, satisfied as Gennie bit into one. "Young girl like you might get lonely away out here."

Gennie shook her head as she swallowed. "No, I like the solitude for painting."

"You do the pictures hanging in the front room?"

"Yes, I hope you don't mind that I hung them."

"Always had a partiality for pictures. You do good work."

Gennie grinned, as pleased with the simple statement as she would have been with a rave review. "Thank you. I plan to do quite a bit of painting around Windy Point—more than I had expected at first," she added, thinking of Grant. "If I decided to stay an extra few weeks—"

"You just let me know."

"Good." Gennie watched as the widow broke off a small piece of muffin. "You must know the lighthouse..." Still nibbling, Gennie toyed with exactly what information she wanted and how to get it.

"Charlie Dees used to keep that station," Mrs. Lawrence told her. "Him and his missus had it since I was a girl. Use radar now, but my father and his father had that light to keep them off the rocks."

There were stories here, Gennie thought. Ones she'd like to hear, but for now it was the present keeper who interested her.

"I met the man who lives there now," she said casually over the rim of her coffee cup. "I'm going to do some painting out there. It's a wonderful spot."

The widow's stiff straight brows rose. "You tell him?"

So they knew him in town, Gennie thought with a mental sniff. "We came to an...agreement of sorts."

"Young Campbell's been there near on to five years." The widow speculated on the gleam in Gennie's eyes, but didn't comment on it. "Keeps to himself. Sent a few out-of-towners on their way quick enough."

"No doubt," Gennie murmured. "He's not a friendly sort."

"Stays out of trouble." The widow gave Gennie a quick, shrewd look. "Nice-looking boy. Hear he's been out with the men on the boats a time or two, but does more watching than talking."

Confused, Gennie swallowed the last of the muffin. "Doesn't he fish for a living?"

"Don't know what he does, but he pays his bills right enough."

Gennie frowned, more intrigued than she wanted to be. "That's odd, I got the impression..." Of what? she asked herself. "I don't suppose he gets a lot of mail," she hazarded.

The widow gave her wispy smile again. "Gets his due," she said simply. "I thank you for the coffee, Miss Grandeau," she added, rising. "And I'm happy to have you stay here as you please."

"Thank you." Knowing she had to be satisfied with the bare snips of information, Gennie rose with her. "I hope you'll come back again, Mrs. Lawrence."

Nodding, the widow made her way back to the front door. "You let me know if you have any problems. When the weather turns, you'll be needing the furnace. It's sound enough mind, but noisier than some."

"I'll remember. Thanks."

Gennie watched her walk to her car and thought about Grant. He wasn't one of them, she mused, but she had sensed a certain reserved affection for him in Mrs. Lawrence's tone. He kept to himself, and that was something the people of Windy Point would respect. Five years, she thought as she wandered back for her paints. A long time to seclude yourself in a lighthouse...doing what?

With a shrug, she gathered her gear. What he did wasn't her concern. Making him crawl a bit was.

The only meal Grant ate with regularity was breakfast. After that, he grabbed what he wanted when he wanted—or when his work permitted. He'd eaten at dawn only because he couldn't sleep, then had gone out on his boat only because he couldn't work. Gennie, tucked into bed two miles away, had managed to interfere with his two most basic activities.

Normally, he would have enjoyed the early run at sea, catching the rosy light with the fishermen and facing the chill dawn air. He would try his luck, and if it was good, have his catch for dinner. If it was bad, he'd broil a steak or open a can.

He hadn't enjoyed his outing this morning, because he had wanted to sleep—then he'd wanted to work. His mood hadn't been tuned to fishing, and the diversion hadn't been a success. The sun had still been low in the sky when he'd returned.

It was high now, but Grant's mood was little better than it had been. Only the discipline he'd imposed on himself over the years kept him at his drawing board, perfecting and refining the strip he'd started the day before.

She'd thrown him off schedule, he thought grimly. And she was running around inside his head. Grant often let people do just that, but they were *his* people, and he controlled them. Gennie refused to stay in character.

Geneviève, he thought, as he meticulously inked in Veronica's long, lush hair. He'd admired her work, its lack of gimmickry, its basic class. She painted with style, and the hint, always the hint of a raging passion underneath a misty overlay of fancy. Her paintings asked you to pretend, to imagine, to believe in something lovely. Grant had never found any fault with that.

He remembered seeing one of her landscapes, one of the bayou scenes that often figured prominently in her showings. The shadows had promised secrets, the dusky blue light a night full of possibilities. There'd been a fog over the water that had made him think of muffled whispers. The tiny house hanging over the river hadn't seemed ramshackle, but lovely in a faded, yesterday way. The serenity of the painting had appealed to him, the clever lighting she'd used had amused him. He could remember being disappointed that the work had already been sold. He wouldn't have even asked the price.

The passion that often lurked around the edges of her works was a subtle contrast to the serenity of her subjects. The fancy had always been uppermost.

She got enough passion in her personal life, he remembered as his mouth tightened. If he hadn't met her, hadn't touched her, he would have kept to the opinion that ninety percent of the things printed about her were just what she had said. Tripe.

But now all he could think was that any man who could get close to Genviève Grandeau would want her. And that the passion that simmered in her paintings, simmered in her equally. She knew she could make a slave out of a man, he thought, and forced himself to complete his drawing of Veronica. She knew it and enjoyed it.

Grant set down his brush a moment and flexed his fingers. Still, he had the satisfaction of knowing he'd turned her aside.

Turned her aside, hell, he thought with a mirthless laugh. If he'd done that he wouldn't be sitting here remembering how she'd been like a fire in his arms—hot, restless, dangerous. He wouldn't be remembering how his mind had gone blank one instant and then had been filled—with only her.

A siren? By God, yes, he thought savagely. It was easy to imagine her smiling and singing and luring a man toward some rocky coast. But not him. He wasn't a man to be bewitched by a seductive voice and a pair of alluring eyes. After his parting shot, he doubted she'd be back in any case. Though he glanced toward the window, Grant refused to go to it. He picked up his brush and worked for another hour, with Gennie teasing the back of his mind.

Satisfied that he had finished the strip on schedule after all, Grant cleaned his brushes. Because the next one was already formed in his mind, his mood was better. With a meticulousness that carried over into no other area of his life, he set his studio to rights. Tools were replaced in a precise manner in and on the glass-topped cabinet beside him. Bottles and jars were wiped clean, tightly capped, and stored. His copy would remain on the drawing board until well dried.

Taking his time, Grant went down to rummage in the kitchen for some food while he kept the portable radio on, filling him in on whatever was going on in the outside world.

A mention of the Ethics Committee, and a senator Grant could never resist satirizing, gave him an angle for another strip. It was true that his use of recognizable names and faces, often in politics, caused some papers to place his work on the editorial page. Grant didn't care where they put it, as long as his point got across. Caricaturing politicians had become a habit when he'd been a child—one he'd never had the least inclination to break.

Leaning against the counter, idly depleting a bag of peanut butter cookies, Grant listened to the rest of the report. An awareness of trends, of moods, of events was as essential to his art as pen and ink. He'd remember what he'd need when the time came to use it. For now it was filed and stored in the back of his mind and he wanted air and sunshine.

He'd go out, Grant told himself, not because he expected to see Gennie—but because he expected not to.

Of course, she was there, but he wanted to believe the surge he felt was annoyance. It was always annoyance—never pleasure—that he felt when he found someone infringing on his solitude.

It wouldn't be much trouble to ignore her.... The wind had her hair caught in its dragging fingers, lifting it from her neck. He could simply go the other way and walk north on the beach.... The sun slanted over the skin of her bare arms and face and had it gleaming. If he turned his back and moved down the other side of the cliff, he'd forget she was even there.

Swearing under his breath, Grant went toward her.

Gennie had seen him, of course, the moment he stepped out. Her brush had only hesitated for a moment before she'd continued to paint. If her pulse had scrambled a bit, she told herself it was only the anticipation of the battle she was looking forward to engaging in—and winning. Because she knew she couldn't afford to keep going now that her concentration was broken, she tapped the handle of her brush to her lips and viewed what she'd done that morning.

The sketch on the canvas gave her precisely what she wanted. The colors she'd already mixed satisfied her. She began to hum, lightly, as she heard Grant draw closer.

"So..." Gennie tilted her head, as if to study the canvas from a different angle. "You decided to come out of your cave."

Grant stuck his hands in his pockets and deliberately stood where he couldn't see her work. "You didn't strike me as the kind of woman who asked for trouble."

Barely moving the angle of her head, Gennie slid her eyes up to his. Her smile was very faint, and very taunting. "I suppose that makes you a poor judge of character, doesn't it?"

The look was calculated to arouse, but knowing it didn't make any difference. He felt the first kindling of desire spread low in his stomach. "Or you a fool," he murmured.

"I told you I'd be back, Grant." She allowed her gaze to drift briefly to his mouth. "Generally I try to—follow through. Would you like to see what I've done?"

He told himself he didn't give a hang about the painting or about her. "No."

Gennie moved her mouth into a pout. "Oh, and I thought you were such an art connoisseur." She set down her brush and ran a hand leisurely through her hair. "What are you, Grant Campbell?" Her eyes were mocking and alluring.

"What I choose to be."

"Fortunate for you." She rose. Taking her time, she drew off the short-sleeved smock and dropped it on the rock beside her. She watched his face as his eyes traveled over her, then ran a lazy finger down his shirtfront. "Shall I tell you what I see?" He didn't answer, but his eyes stayed on hers. Gennie wondered if she pressed her hand to his heart if the beat would be fast and unsteady. "A loner," she continued, "with the face of a buccaneer and the hands of a poet. And the manners," she added with a soft laugh, "of a lout. It seems to me that the manners are all you've had the choice about."

It was difficult to resist the gleam of challenge in her eyes or the promise in those soft, full lips that smiled with calculated feminine insolence. "If you like," Grant said mildly while he kept the hands that itched to touch her firmly in his pockets.

"I can't say I do." Gennie walked a few steps away, close enough to the cliff edge so that the spray nearly reached her. "Then again, your manners add a rather rough-and-ready appeal." She glanced over her shoulder. "I don't suppose a woman always wants a gentleman. You wouldn't be a man who looks for a lady."

With the sea behind her, reflecting the color of her eyes, she looked more a part of it than ever. "Is that what you are, Geneviève?"

She laughed, pleased with the frustration and fury she read in his eyes. "It depends," she said, deliberately mimicking him, "on whether it's useful or not."

Grant came to her then but resisted the desire to shake her until her teeth rattled. Their bodies were close, so that little more than the wind could pass between them. "What the hell are you trying to do?"

She gave him an innocent stare. "Why, have a conversation. I suppose you're out of practice."

He glared, narrowed-eyed, then turned away. "I'm going for a walk," he muttered.

"Lovely." Gennie slipped her arm through his. "I'll go with you."

"I didn't ask you," Grant said flatly, stopping again.

"Oh." Gennie batted her eyes. "You're trying to charm me by being rude again. It's so difficult to resist."

A grin tugged at his mouth before he controlled it. There was no one he laughed at more easily than himself. "All right, then." There was a gleam in his eyes she didn't quite trust. "Come on."

Grant walked swiftly, without deference to the difference in their strides. Determined to make him suffer before the afternoon was over, Gennie trotted to keep up. After they'd circled the lighthouse, Grant started down the cliff with the confidence of long experience. Gennie took a long look at the steep drop, at the rock ledges Grant walked down with no more care than if they'd been steps. Below, the surf churned and battered at the shoreline. She wasn't about to be intimidated, Gennie reminded herself. He'd just love that. Taking a deep breath, she started after him.

For the first few feet her heart was in her throat. She'd really make him suffer if she fell and broke her neck. Then she began to enjoy it. The sea grew louder with the descent. Salt spray tingled along her skin. Doubtless there was a simpler way down, but at the moment she wouldn't have looked for it.

Grant reached the bottom in time to turn and see Gennie scrambling down the last few feet. He'd wanted to believe she'd still be up on the cliff, yet somehow he'd known better. She was no hot-house magnolia no matter how much he'd like to have tossed her in that category. She was much too vital to be admired from a distance.

Instinctively, he reached for her hand to help her down. Gennie brushed against him on the landing, then stood, head tilted back, daring him to do something about it. Her scent rushed to his senses. Before, she'd only smelled of the rain. This was just as subtle, but infinitely more sensuous. She smelled of night in the full light of the afternoon, and of all those whispering, murmuring promises that bloomed after sundown.

Infuriated that he could be lured by such an obvious tactic, Grant released her. Without a word he started down the narrow, rocky beach where the sea boomed and echoed and the gulls screamed. Smug and confident with her early success, Gennie moved with him.

Oh, I'm getting to you, Grant Campbell. And I haven't even started.

"Is this what you do with your time when you're not locked in your secret tower?"

"Is this what you do with your time when you're not hitting the hot spots on Bourbon Street?"

Tossing back her hair, Gennie deliberately slipped her arm through his again. "Oh, we talked enough about me yesterday. Tell me about Grant Campbell. Are you a mad scientist conducting terrifying experiments under secret government contract?"

He turned his head, then gave her an odd smile. "At the moment I'm stamp collecting."

That puzzled her enough that she forgot the game and frowned. "Why do I feel there's some grain of truth in that?"

With a shrug, Grant continued to walk, wondering why he didn't shake her off and go on his way alone. When he came here, he always came alone. Walks along this desolate, rocky beach were the only time other than sleep that he allowed his mind to empty. There where the waves crashed like thunder and the ground was hard and unforgiving was his haven against his own thoughts and self-imposed pressure. He'd never allowed anyone to join him there, not even his own creations. He wanted to feel the sense of intrusion he'd expected with Gennie at his side; instead he felt something very close to contentment.

"A secret place," Gennie murmured.

Distracted, Grant glanced down at her. "What?"

"This." Gennie gestured with her free hand. "This is a secret place." Bending she picked up a shell, pitted by the ocean, dried like a bone in the sun. "My grandmother has a beautiful old plantation house filled with antiques and silk pillows. There's a room off the attic upstairs. It's gloomy and dusty. There's a broken rocker in there and a box full of perfectly useless things. I could sit up there for hours.'' Bringing her gaze back to his, she smiled. ''I've never been able to resist a secret place.''

Grant remembered, suddenly and vividly, a tiny storeroom in his parents' home in Georgetown. He'd closeted himself in there for hours at a stretch with stacks of comic books and a sketch pad. ''It's only a secret if nobody knows about it.''

She laughed, slipping her hand into his without any thought. ''Oh, no, it can still be a secret with two—sometimes a better secret.'' She stopped to watch a gull swoop low over the water. ''What are those islands out there?''

Disturbed, because her hand felt as though it belonged in his, Grant scowled out to sea. ''Hunks of rock mostly.''

''Oh.'' Gennie sent him a desolate look. ''No bleached bones or pieces of eight?''

The grin snuck up on him. ''There be talk of a skull that moans when a storm's brewing,'' he told her, slipping into a thick Down East cadence.

''Whose?'' Gennie demanded, ready for whatever story he could conjure.

''A seaman's,'' Grant improvised. ''He lusted after his captain's woman. She had the eyes of a sea-witch and hair like midnight.'' Despite himself Grant took a handful of Gennie's while the rest tossed in the wind. ''She tempted him, made him soft, wicked promises if he'd steal the gold and the longboat. When he did, because she was a woman who could drive a man to murder with a look, she went with him.'' Grant felt her hair tangle around his fingers as though it had a life of its own.

"So he rowed for two days and two nights, knowing when they came to land he'd have her. But when they spotted the coast, she drew out a saber and lopped off his head. Now his skull sits on the rocks and moans in frustrated desire."

Amused, Gennie tilted her head. "And the woman?"

"Invested her gold, doubled her profits, and became a pillar of the community."

Laughing, Gennie began to walk with him again. "The moral seems to be never trust a woman who makes you promises."

"Certainly not a beautiful one."

"Have you had your head lopped off, Grant?"

He gave a short, appreciative laugh. "No."

"A pity." She sighed. "I suppose that means you make a habit of resisting temptation."

"It's not necessary to resist it," he countered. "As long as you keep one eye open."

"There's no romance in that," Gennie complained.

"I've other uses for my head, thanks."

She shot him a thoughtful look. "Stamp collecting?"

"For one."

They walked in silence again while the sea crashed close beside them. On the other side the rocks rose like a wall. Far out on the water there were dots of boats. That one sign of humanity only added to the sense of space and aloneness.

"Where did you come from?" she asked impulsively.

"The same place you did."

It took her a minute, then she chuckled. "I don't mean biologically. Geographically."

He shrugged, trying not to be pleased she had caught on so quickly. "South of here."

"Oh, well that's specific," she muttered, then tried again. "What about family? Do you have family?"

He stopped to study her. "Why?"

With an exaggerated sigh, Gennie shook her head. "This is called making friendly conversation. It's a new trend that's catching on everywhere."

"I'm a noncomformist."

"No! Really?"

"You do that wide-eyed, guileless look very well, Genviève."

"Thank you." She turned the shell over in her hand, then looked up at him with a slow smile. "I'll tell you something about my family, just to give you a running start." She thought for a moment, then hit on something she thought he'd relate to. "I have a cousin, a few times removed. I've always thought he was the most fascinating member of the family tree, though you couldn't call him a Grandeau."

"What would you call him?"

"The black sheep," she said with relish. "He did things his own way, never giving a damn about what anyone thought. I heard stories about him from time to time—though I wasn't meant to—and it wasn't until I was a grown woman that I met him. I'm happy to say we took to each other within minutes and have kept in touch over the last couple of years. He'd lived his life by his wits, and done quite well—which didn't sit well with some of the more staid members of the family. Then he confounded everyone by getting married."

"To an exotic dancer."

"No." She laughed, pleased that he was interested enough to joke. "To someone absolutely suitable—intelligent, well bred, wealthy—" She rolled her eyes. "The black sheep, who'd spent some time in jail, gambled his way into a fortune, had outdone them all." With a laugh, Gennie thought of the Comanche Blade. Cousin Justin had indeed outdone them all. And he didn't even bother to thumb his nose.

"I love a happy ending," Grant said dryly.

With her eyes narrowed, Gennie turned to him. "Don't you know that the less you tell someone, the more they want to know? You're better off to make something up than to say nothing at all."

"I'm the youngest of twelve children of two South African missionaries," he said with such ease, she very nearly believed him. "When I was six, I wandered into the jungle and was taken in by a pride of lions. I still have a penchant for zebra meat. Then when I was eighteen, I was captured by hunters and sold to a circus. For five years I was the star of the sideshow."

"The Lion Boy," Gennie put it.

"Naturally. One night during a storm the tent caught fire. In the confusion I escaped. Living off the land, I wandered the country—stealing a few chickens now and again. Eventually an old hermit took me in after I'd saved him from a grizzly."

"With your bare hands," Gennie added.

"I'm telling the story," he reminded her. "He taught me to read and write. On his deathbed he told me where he'd buried his life savings—a quarter million in gold bullion. After giving him the Viking funeral he'd requested, I had to decide whether to be a stockbroker or go back to the wilderness."

"So you decided against Wall Street, came here, and began to collect stamps."

"That's about it."

"Well," Gennie said after a moment. "With a boring story like that, I can see why you keep it to yourself."

"You asked," Grant pointed out.

"You might have made something up."

"No imagination."

She laughed then and leaned her head on his shoulder. "No, I can see you have a very literal mind."

Her laugh rippled along his skin, and the casual intimacy of her head against his shoulder shot straight down to the soles of his feet. He should shake her off, Grant told himself. He had no business walking here with her and enjoying it. "I've got things to do," he said abruptly. "We can go up this way."

It was the change in his tone that reminded Gennie she'd come there for a purpose, and the purpose was not to wind up liking him.

The way up was easier than the way down, she noted as he turned toward what was now a slope rather than a cliff. Though his fingers loosened on hers, she held on, shooting him a smile that had him muttering under his breath as he helped her climb. Thinking quickly, she stuck the shell in her back pocket. When they neared the top, Gennie held her other hand out to him. With her eyes narrowed a bit against the sun, her hair flowing down her back, she looked up at him. Swearing, Grant grabbed her other hand and hauled her up the last few feet.

On level ground she stayed close, her body just brushing his as their hands remained linked. His breath had stayed even during the climb, but now it came unsteadily. Feeling a surge of satisfaction, Gennie gave him a slow, lazy smile.

"Going back to your stamps?" she murmured. Deliberately, she leaned closer to brush her lips over his chin. "Enjoy yourself." Drawing her hands from his, Gennie turned. She'd taken three steps before he grabbed her arm. Though her heart began to thud, she looked over her shoulder at him. "Want something?" she asked in a low, amused voice.

She could see it on his face—the struggle for control. And in his eyes she could see a flare of desire that had her throat going dry. No, she wasn't going to back down now, she insisted. She'd finish out the game. When he yanked her against him, she told herself it wasn't fear she felt, it wasn't passion. It was self-gratification.

"It seems you do," she said with a laugh, and slid her hands up his back.

When his mouth crushed down on hers, her mind spun. All thoughts of purpose, all thoughts of revenge vanished. It was as it had been the first time—the passion, and over the passion a rightness, and with the rightness a storm of confused needs and longings and wishes. Opening to him was so natural she did so without thought, and with a simplicity that made him groan as he drew her closer.

His tongue skimmed over her lips then tangled with hers as his hands roamed to mold her hips. Strong hands—she'd known they'd be strong. Her skin tingled with the image of being touched without barriers even as her mouth sought to take all he could give her through a kiss alone. She strained against him, offering, demanding, and it seemed he couldn't give or take fast enough to satisfy either of them. His mouth ravaged, but hers wouldn't surrender. What she drew out of him excited them both.

It wasn't until she began to feel the weakness that Gennie remembered to fear. This wasn't what she'd come for... Was it? No, she wouldn't believe she'd come to feel this terrifying pleasure, this aching, gnawing need to give what she'd never given before. Panic rose and she struggled against it in a way she knew she'd never be able to struggle against desire. She had to stop him, and herself. If he held her much longer, she would melt, and melting, lose.

Drawing on what was left of her strength she pulled back, determined not to show either the passion or the fear that raced through her. "Very nice," she murmured, praying he wouldn't notice how breathless her voice was. "Though your technique's a bit—rough for my taste."

His breath came quick and fast. Grant didn't speak, knowing if he did madness would pour out. For the second time she'd emptied him out then filled him again with herself. Need for her, raw, exclusive, penetrating, ripped through him as he stared into her eyes and waited for it to abate. It didn't.

He was stronger than she was, he told himself as he gathered her shirtfront in his hand. Her heart thudded against his knuckles. There was nothing to stop him from... He dropped his hand as though she'd scalded him. No one pushed him to that, he thought furiously while she continued to stare up at him. No one.

"You're walking on dangerous ground, Genviève," he said softly.

She tossed back her head. "I'm very sure-footed." With a parting smile, she turned, counting each step as she went back to her canvas. Perhaps her hands weren't steady as she packed up her gear. Perhaps her blood roared in her ears. But she'd won the first round. She let out a deep breath as she heard the door to the lighthouse slam shut.

The first round, she repeated, wishing she wasn't looking forward quite so much to the next one.

Chapter Five

Grant managed to avoid Gennie for three days. She came back to paint every morning, and though she worked for hours, she never saw a sign of him. The lighthouse was silent, its windows winking blankly in the sun.

Once his boat was gone when she arrived and hadn't returned when she lost the light she wanted. She was tempted to go down the cliff and walk along the beach where he had taken her. She found she could have more easily strolled into his house uninvited than gone to that one particular spot without his knowledge. Even had she wanted to paint there, the sense of trespassing would have forbidden it.

She painted in peace, assured that since she had gotten her own back with Grant she wouldn't think of him. But the painting itself kept him lodged in her mind. She would never be able to see that spot, on canvas or in reality, and not see him. It was his, as surely as if he'd been hewed from the rocks or tossed up by the sea. She could feel the force of his personality as she guided her brush, and the challenge of it as she struggled to put what should have only been nature's mood onto canvas.

But it wouldn't only be nature's, she discovered as she painted sea and surf. Though his form wouldn't be on the canvas, his substance would. Gennie had always felt a particle of her own soul went into each one of her canvases. In this one she would capture a part of Grant's as well. Neither of them had a choice.

Somehow knowing it drove her to create something with force and muscle. The painting excited her. She knew she'd been meant to paint that view, and to paint it well. And she knew when it was done, she would give it to Grant. Because it could never belong to anyone else.

It wouldn't be a token of affection, she told herself, or an offer of friendship. It was simply something that had to be done. She'd never be able, in good conscience, to sell that canvas. And if she kept it herself, he'd haunt her. So before she left Windy Point, she would make him a gift of it. Perhaps, in her way, she would then haunt him.

Her mornings were filled with an urgency to finish it, an urgency she had to block again and again unless she miss something vital in the process. Gennie knew it was imperative to move slowly, to absorb everything around her and give it to the painting. In the afternoons she forced herself to pack up so that she wouldn't work longer than she should and ignore the changing light.

She sketched her inlet and planned a watercolor. She fretted for morning so that she could go back to the sea.

Her restlessness drove her to town. It was time to make some sketches there, to decide what she would paint and in what medium. She told herself she needed to see people again to keep her mind from focusing so continually on Grant.

In the midafternoon, Windy Point was sleepy and quiet. Boats were out to sea, and a hazy summer heat shimmered in the air. She saw a woman sitting on her porch stringing the last of the season's beans while a toddler plucked at the clover in the yard.

Gennie parked her car at the end of the road and began to walk. She could sketch the buildings, the gardens. She could gather impressions that would bring them to life again when she began to paint. This was a different world from the force at Windy Point Station, different yet from the quiet inlet behind her cottage, but they were all connected. The sea touched all of them in different ways.

She wandered, glad she had come though the voices she heard were voices of strangers. It was a town she'd remember more clearly than any of the others she'd visited on her tour of New England. But it was the sea that continued to tug at her underneath it all—and the man who lived there.

When would she see him again? Gennie wondered, forced to admit that she missed him. She missed the scowl and the curt words, the quick grin and surprising humor, the light of amused cynicism she caught in his eyes from time to time. And though it was the hardest to admit, she missed that furious passion he'd brought to her so suddenly.

Leaning against the side of a building, she wondered if there would be another man somewhere who would touch her that way. She couldn't imagine one. She'd never looked for a knight in armor—they were simply too much trouble, expecting a helpless damsel in return. Helpless she would never be, and chivalry, for the most part, got in the way of an intelligent relationship. Grant Campbell, Gennie mused, would never be chivalrous, and a helpless female would infuriate him.

Remembering their first meeting, she chuckled. No, he didn't care to be put out by a lady in distress anymore than she cared to be one. She supposed, on both parts, it went back to a fierce need for independence.

No, he wasn't looking for a lady, and while she hadn't been looking for a knight, she hadn't been searching out ogres, either. Gennie thought Grant came very close to fitting into that category. While she enjoyed men's company, she didn't want one tangling up her life—at least not until she was ready. And she certainly didn't want to be involved with an ogre—they were entirely too unpredictable. Who knew when they'd just swallow you whole?

Shaking her head, she glanced down, surprised to see that she'd not only been thinking of Grant, but had been sketching him. Lips pursed, Gennie lifted the pad for a critical study. A good likeness, she decided. His eyes were narrowed a bit, dark and intense on the point of anger. His brows were lowered, forming that faint vertical line of temper between them. She'd captured that lean face with its planes and shadows, the aristocratic nose and unruly hair. And his mouth...

The little jolt of response wasn't surprising, but it was unwelcomed. She'd drawn his mouth as she'd seen it before it came down on hers—the sensuousness, the ruthlessness. Yes, she could taste that stormy flavor even now, standing in the quiet town with the scent of fish and aging flowers around her.

Carefully closing the book, Gennie reminded herself she'd be much better off sticking to the buildings she'd come to draw. With the pencil stuck behind her ear, Gennie crossed the road to go into the post office. The skinny teenager she remembered from her first trip through the town turned to goggle at her when she entered. As she walked up to the counter, she smiled at him, then watched his Adam's apple bob up and down.

"Will." Mrs. Lawrence plunked letters down on the counter. "You'd best be getting Mr. Fairfield his mail before you lose your job."

"Yes, ma'am." He scooped at the letters while he continued to stare at Gennie. When he dropped the lot of them on the floor, Gennie bent to help him and sent him into a blushing attack of stutters.

"Will Turner," Mrs. Lawrence repeated with the pitch of an impatient schoolteacher. "Gather up those letters and be on your way."

"You missed one, Will," Gennie said kindly, then handed the envelope to him as his jaw went slack. Face pink, eyes glued to hers, Will stumbled to the door and out.

Mrs. Lawrence gave a dry chuckle. "Be lucky he doesn't fall off the curb."

"I suppose I should be flattered," Gennie considered. "I don't remember having that effect on anyone before."

"Awkward age for a boy when he starts noticing females is shaped a bit different."

With a laugh, Gennie leaned on the counter. "I wanted to thank you again for coming by the other day. I've been painting out at the lighthouse and haven't been into town."

Mrs. Lawrence glanced down at the sketchbook Gennie had set on the counter. "Doing some drawing here?"

"Yes." On impulse, Gennie opened the book and flipped through. "It was the town that interested me right away—the sense of permanence and purpose."

Cool-eyed, the widow paged through the book while Gennie nibbled on her lip and waited for the verdict. "Ayah," she said at length. "You know what you're about." With one finger, she pushed back a sheet, then studied Gennie's sketch of Grant. "Looks a bit fierce," she decided as the wispy smile touched her mouth.

"*Is* a bit for my thinking," Gennie countered.

"Ayah, well there be a woman who like a touch of vinegar in a man." She gave another dry chuckle and for once her eyes were more friendly than shrewd. "I be one of them." With a glance over Gennie's shoulder, the widow closed the book. "Afternoon, Mr. Campbell."

For a moment Gennie goggled at the widow much as Will had goggled at her. Recovering, she laid a hand on the now closed book.

"Afternoon, Mrs. Lawrence." When he came to stand at the counter beside her, Gennie caught the scent of the sea on him. "Genviève," he said, giving her a long, enigmatic look.

He'd wondered how long he could stand it before he saw her up close again. There'd been too many times in the past three days that he hadn't been able to resist the urge to go to his studio window and watch her paint. All that had stopped him from going down to her was the knowledge that if he touched her again, he'd be heading down a road he'd never turn back from. As yet he was uncertain what was at the end of it.

A picture of the blushing, stuttering teenager ran through her mind and straightened Gennie's spine. "Hello, Grant." When she smiled, she was careful to bank down the warmth and make up for it with mockery. "I thought you were hibernating."

"Been busy," he said easily. "Didn't know you were still around." That gave him the satisfaction of seeing annoyance dart into her eyes before she controlled it.

"I'll be around for some time yet."

Mrs. Lawrence slid a thick bundle of mail on the counter, then followed it with a stack of newspapers. Gennie caught the Chicago return address of the top letter and the banner of the *Washington Post* before Grant scooped everything up. "Thanks."

With a frown between her brows, Gennie watched him walk out. There must have been a dozen letters *and* a dozen newspapers. Letters from Chicago, a Washington paper for a man who lived on a deserted cliff outside a town that didn't even boast a stoplight. What in the hell...

"Fine-looking young man," Mrs. Lawrence commented behind Gennie's back.

With a mumbled answer, Gennie started for the door. "Bye, Mrs. Lawrence."

Mrs. Lawrence tapped a finger on the counter thinking there hadn't been such tugging and pulling in the air since the last storm. Maybe another one was brewing.

Puzzled, Gennie began to walk again. It wasn't any of her business why some odd recluse received so much mail. For all she knew, he might only come into town to pick it up once a month...but that had been yesterday's paper. With a brisk shake of her head, she struggled against curiosity. The real point was that she'd been able to get a couple shots in—even if he'd had a bull's-eye for her.

She loitered at the corner, doing another quick sketch while she reminded herself that instead of thinking of him, she should be thinking what provisions she needed before she headed back to the cottage.

But she was restless again. The sense of order and place she'd found after an hour in town had vanished the moment he'd walked into the post office. She wanted to find that feeling again before she went back to spend the night alone.

Aimlessly, she wandered down the road, pausing now and then at a store window. She was nearly to the edge of town when she remembered the churchyard. She'd sketch there until she was tired enough to go home.

A truck rattled by, perhaps the third vehicle Gennie had seen in an hour. After waiting for it, she crossed the road. She passed the small, uneven plot of the cemetery, listening to the quiet. The grass was high enough to bend in the breeze. Overhead a flock of gulls flew by, calling out on their way to the sea.

The paint on the high fence was rusted and peeling. Queen Anne's lace grew stubbornly between the posts. The church itself was small and white with a single stained-glass panel at the V of the roof. Other windows were clear glass and paned, and the door itself was sturdy and scarred with time. Gennie walked to the side and sat where the grass had been recently tended. She could smell it.

Fleetingly she wondered how it was possible one tiny scrap on the map could have so much that demanded to be painted. She could easily spend six months there rather than six weeks and never capture all she wanted to.

The restlessness evaporated as she began to sketch. Perhaps she wouldn't be able to transfer everything into oils or watercolor before she left, but she'd have the sketches. In months to come, she could use them to go back to Windy Point when she felt the need for it.

She'd turned over the page to start a second sketch when a shadow fell over her. A quick fluctuation of her pulse, a swift warmth on her skin. She knew who stood behind her. Shading her eyes, she looked up at Grant. "Well," she said lightly, "twice in one day."

"Small town." He gestured toward her pad. "You finished out at the station?"

"No, the light's wrong this time of day for what I want there."

It was annoyance he was supposed to feel, not relief. Casually, he dropped to the grass beside her. "So now you're going to immortalize Windy Point."

"In my own small way," she said dryly, and started to sketch again. Was she glad he had come? Hadn't she known, somehow, he would? "Still playing with stamps?"

"No, I've taken up classical music." He only smiled when she turned to study him. "You'd have been reared on that, I imagine. A little Brahms after dinner."

"I favored Chopin." She tapped her pencil on her chin. "What did you do with your mail?"

"I stowed it."

"I didn't notice your truck."

"I brought the boat." Taking the sketchbook, he flipped through to the front.

"For someone who's so keen on privacy," she began heatedly, "you have little respect when it belongs to someone else."

"Yeah." Unceremoniously, he shoved her hand away when she reached for the pad. While she simmered, Grant went through the book, pausing, then going on until he came to the sketch of himself. He studied it a moment, wordlessly, then surprised Gennie by grinning. "Not bad," he decided.

"I'm overwhelmed by your flattery."

He considered her a moment, then acted on impulse. "One deserves another."

Plucking the pencil out of her fingers, he turned the pages over until he came to a blank one. To her astonishment, he began to draw with the easy confidence of long practice. Mouth open, she stared at him while he whistled between his teeth and looped lines and curves onto the paper. His eyes narrowed a moment as he added some shading, then he tossed the book back into her lap. Gennie gave him a long, last stare before she looked down.

It was definitely her—in clever, merciless caricature. Her eyes were slanted—exaggerated, almost predatory, her cheekbones an aristocratic slash, her chin a stubborn point. With her mouth just parted and her head tilted back, he'd given her the expression of royalty mildly displeased. Gennie studied it for a full ten seconds before she burst into delighted laughter.

"You pig!" she said and laughed again. "I look like I'm about to have a minion beheaded."

He might have been saved if she'd gotten angry, been insulted. Then he could have written her off as vain and humorless and not worth his notice—at least he could have tried. Now with her laughter bouncing on the air and her eyes alive with it, Grant stepped off the cliff.

"Gennie." He murmured her name as his hand reached up to touch her face. Her laughter died.

What she would have said if her throat hadn't closed, she didn't know. She thought the air went very still very suddenly. The only movement seemed to be the fingers that brushed the hair back from her face, the only sound her own uneven breath. When he lowered his face toward hers, she didn't move but waited.

He hesitated, though the pause was too short to measure, before he touched his mouth to hers. Gentle, questioning, it sent a line of fire down her spine. For him, too, she realized, as his fingers tightened, briefly, convulsively, on her neck before they relaxed again. He must be feeling, as she did, that sudden urgent thrust of power that was followed by a dazed kind of weakness.

Floating...were people meant to float like this? Limitless, mindless. How could she have known one man's lips could bring such an endless variety of sensations when touched to hers? Perhaps she'd never been kissed before and only thought she had. Perhaps she had only imagined another man casually brushing her mouth with his. Because this was real.

She could taste—warm breath. She could feel—lips soft, yet firm and knowing. She could smell—that subtle scent on him that meant wind and sea. She could see—his face, blurred and close when her lashes drifted up to assure her. And when he moaned her name, she heard him.

Her answer was to melt, slowly, luxuriously against him. With the melting came a pain, unexpected and sharp enough to make her tremble. How could there be pain, she wondered dazedly, when her body was so truly at peace? Yet it came again on a wave that rocked her. Some lucid part of her mind reminded her that love hurt.

But no. She tried to shake off the pain, and the knowledge it brought her even as her lips clung to his. She wasn't falling in love, not now, not with him. That wasn't what she wanted.... What did she want? *Him*.

The answer came so clearly, so simply. It drove her into panic.

"Grant, no." She drew away, but the hand on her face slid to the back of her neck and held her still.

"No, what?" His voice was very quiet, with rough edges.

"I didn't intend—we shouldn't be—I didn't... Oh!" She shut her eyes, frustrated that she could be reduced to stammering confusion.

"Why don't you run that by me again?"

The trace of humor in his voice had her springing to her feet. She wasn't lightheaded, she told herself. She'd simply sat too long and rose too quickly. "Look, this is hardly the place for this kind of thing."

"What kind of thing?" he countered, rising, too, but with a lazy ease that moved muscle by muscle. "We were only kissing. That's more popular than making friendly conversation. Kissing you's become a habit." He reached out for her hair, then let it drift through his spread fingers. "I don't break them easily."

"In this case—" she paused to even her breathing "—I think you should make an exception."

He studied her, trying to make light of something that had struck him down to the bone. "You're quite a mix, Genvière. The practiced seductress one minute, the confused virgin the next. You know how to fascinate a man."

Pride moved automatically to shield her. "Some men are more easily fascinated than others."

"True enough." Grant wasn't sure just what emotion was working through him, but he knew it wasn't comfortable. "Damn if I won't be glad to see the last of you," he muttered.

Listening to the sound of his retreating footsteps, Gennie bent to pick up her sketchbook. By some malicious coincidence, it had fallen open to Grant's face. Gennie scowled at it. "And I'll be glad to see the last of you." She closed the book, made a business of brushing off her jeans, and started to leave the churchyard with quiet dignity.

The hell with it!

"Grant!" She raced down the steps to the sidewalk and tore after him. "Grant, wait!"

With every sign of impatience, he turned and did so. "What?"

A little breathless, she stopped in front of him and wondered what it was she wanted to say. No, she didn't want to see the last of him. If she didn't understand why yet, she felt she was at least entitled to a little time to find out.

"Truce," she decided and held out a hand. When he only stared at her, she gave a quick huff and swallowed another morsel of pride. "Please."

Trapped by the single word, he took the offered hand. "All right." When she would have drawn her hand away, he tightened his grip. "Why?"

"I don't know," Gennie told him with fresh impatience. "Just a wild urge to see if I can get along with an ogre." At the ironic lift of his brow, she sighed. "All right, that was just a quick slip. I take it back."

Idly, he twisted the thin gold chain she wore around her finger. "So, what now?"

What now indeed? Gennie thought as even the brush of his knuckles had her skin humming. She wasn't going to give in to it—but she wasn't going to jump like a scared rabbit either. "Listen, I owe you a meal," she said impulsively. "I'll pay you back, that way we'll have a clean slate."

"How?"

"I'll cook you dinner."

"You've already cooked me breakfast."

"That was your food," Gennie pointed out. Already planning things out, she looked past him into town. "I'll need to pick up a few things."

Grant studied her, considering. "You going to bring them to the lighthouse?"

Oh, no, she thought immediately. She knew better than to trust herself with him there, that close to the sea and the power. "To my cottage. There's a little brick barbecue out back if you like steaks."

What's going on in her mind? he wondered as he watched secret thoughts flicker in her eyes. He knew he'd never be able to resist finding out. "I've been known to choke down a bite or two in my time."

"Okay." She gave a decisive nod and took his hand. "Let's go shopping."

"Wait a minute," Grant began as she pulled him down the sidewalk.

"Oh, don't start complaining already. Where do I buy the steaks?"

"Bayside," Grant said dryly, and brought her up short.

"Oh."

Grinning at her expression, he draped an arm around her shoulder. "Once in a while Leeman's Market gets in a few good cuts of meat."

Gennie shot him a suspicious look. "From where?"

Still grinning, Grant pushed open the market door. "I love a mystery."

Gennie wasn't certain she was amused until she found there was indeed a steak—only one, but sizable enough for two people—and that it was from a nearby farm, authorized and licensed. Satisfied with this, and a bag of fresh salad greens, Gennie drew Grant outside again.

"Okay, now where can I buy a bottle of wine?"

"Fairfield's," he suggested. "He carries the only spirits in town. If you're not too particular about the label."

As they started across the road, a boy biked by, shooting Grant a quick look before he ducked his chin on his chest and pedaled away.

"One of your admirers?" Gennie asked dryly.

"I chased him and three of his friends off the cliffs a few weeks back."

"You're a real sport."

Grant only grinned, remembering his first reaction had been fury at having his peace interrupted, then fear that the four careless boys would break their necks on the rocks. "Ayah," he said, recalling with pleasure the acid tongue-lashing he'd doled out.

"Do you really kick sick dogs?" she asked as she caught the gleam in his eye.

"Only on my own land."

Heaving a hefty sigh, Gennie pushed open the door of Fairfield's store. Across the room, Will immediately dropped the large pot he'd been about to stock on a shelf. Red to the tips of his ears, he left it where it was. "Help you?" His voice cracked painfully on the last word.

"I need a bag of charcoal," Gennie told him as she crossed the room. "And a bottle of wine."

"Charcoal's in the back," he managed, then took a step in retreat as Gennie came closer. His elbow caught a stack of cans and sent them crashing. "What—what size?"

Torn between laughter and sympathy, Gennie swallowed. "Five pounds'll be fine."

"I'll get it." The boy disappeared, and Gennie caught Fairfield's voice demanding what the devil ailed him before she was forced to press a hand to her mouth to hold back the laughter.

Thinking of Macintosh's reaction to Veronica, Grant felt a wave of empathy. "Poor kid's going to be mooning like a puppy for a month. Did you have to smile at him?"

"Really, Grant. He can't be more than fifteen."

"Old enough to break out in a sweat," he commented.

"Hormones," she murmured as she found Fairfield's sparse selection of wine. "They just need time to balance."

Grant's gaze drifted down and focused as she bent over. "It should only take thirty or forty years," he muttered.

Gennie found a domestic burgundy and plucked it from the bottom shelf. "Looks like we feast after all."

Will came back with a bag of charcoal and almost managed not to trip over his own feet. "Brought you some starter, too, in case..." He broke off as his tongue tied itself into knots.

"Oh, thanks." Gennie set the wine on the counter and reached for her wallet.

"You gotta be of age to buy the wine," Will began. Gennie's smile widened and his blush deepened. "Guess you are, huh?"

Unable to resist, Gennie gestured to Grant. "He is."

Enraptured, Will stared at Gennie until she gently asked what the total was. He came to long enough to punch out numbers on the little adding machine, send it into clanking convulsions, and begin again.

"It be five-oh-seven, with—" a long sigh escaped "—tax."

Gennie resisted the urge to pat his cheek and counted out the change into his damp palm. "Thank you, Will."

Will's fingers closed over the nickel and two pennies. "Yes, ma'am."

For the first time the boy's eyes left Gennie's. Grant was struck with a look of such awe and envy, he wasn't sure whether to preen or apologize. In a rare gesture of casual affection, he reached over and squeezed Will's shoulder. "Makes a man want to sit up and beg, doesn't she?" he murmured when Gennie reached the door.

Will sighed. "Ayah." Before Grant could turn, Will plucked at his sleeve. "You gonna have dinner with her and everything?"

Grant lifted a brow but managed to keep his composure. *Everything,* he reminded himself, meant different things to different people. At the moment it conjured up rather provocative images in his brain. "Things are presently unsettled," he murmured, using one of Macintosh's stock phrases. Catching himself, he grinned. "Yeah, we're going to have dinner." And something, he added as he strolled out after Gennie.

"What was all that about?" she demanded.

"Man talk."

"Oh, I beg your pardon."

The way she said it—very antebellum and disdainful—made him laugh and pull her into his arms to kiss her in full view of all of Windy Point. As the embrace lingered on, Grant caught the muffled crash from inside Fairfield's. "Poor Will," he murmured. "I know just how he feels." Humor flashed into his eyes again. "I better start around in the boat if we're going to have dinner...and everything."

Confused by his uncharacteristic lightheartedness, Gennie gave him a long stare. "All right," she said after a moment. "I'll meet you there."

Chapter Six

It was foolish to feel like a girl getting ready for a date. Gennie told herself that as she unlocked the door to the cottage. She'd told herself the same thing as she'd driven away from town...and as she'd turned down the quiet lane.

It was a spur of the moment cookout—two adults, a steak, and a bottle of burgundy that may or may not have been worth the price. A person would have to look hard to find any romance in charcoal, lighter fluid, and some freshly picked greens from a patch in the backyard. Not for the first time, Gennie thought it a pity her imagination was so expansive.

It had undoubtedly been imagination that had brought on that rush of feeling in the churchyard. A little unexpected tenderness, a soft breeze, and she heard bells. Silly.

Gennie set the bags on the kitchen counter and wished she'd bought candles. Candlelight would make even that tidy, practical little kitchen seem romantic. And if she had a radio, there could be music...

Catching herself, Gennie rolled her eyes to the ceiling. What was she thinking of? She'd never had any patience with such obvious, conventional trappings in the first place, and in the second place she didn't *want* a romance with Grant. She'd go halfway toward making a friendship—a very careful friendship—with him, but that was it.

She'd cook dinner for him because she owed him that much. They'd have conversation because she found him interesting despite the thorns. And she'd make very, very certain she didn't end up in his arms again. Whatever part of her longed for a repeat of what had happened between them in the churchyard would have to be overruled by common sense. Grant Campbell was not only basically unpleasant, he was just too complicated. Gennie considered herself too complex a person to be involved with anyone who had so many layers to him.

Gennie grabbed the bag of charcoal and the starter and went into the side yard to set the grill. It was so quiet, she mused, looking around as she ripped the bag open. She'd hear Grant coming long before she saw him.

It was the perfect time for a ride on the water, with the late afternoon shadows lengthening and the heat draining from the day. The light was bland as milk now, and as soothing. She could hear the light lap-slap of water against the pier and the rustle of insects in the high grass on the bank. Then, barely, she heard the faint putt of a distant motor.

Her nerves gathered together so quickly, Gennie nearly dropped the five pounds of briquettes on the ground. When she'd finished being exasperated with herself, she laughed and poured a neat pile of charcoal into the barbecue pit. So this was the coolly sophisticated Geneviève Grandeau, she thought wryly; established member of the art world and genteel New Orleans society, about to drop five pounds of charcoal on her toes because a rude man was going to have dinner with her. How the mighty have fallen.

With a grin, she rolled the bag up and dropped it on the ground. So what? she asked herself before she strolled down to the pier to wait for him.

Grant took the turn into the inlet at a speed that sent water spraying high. Laughing, Gennie stretched on her toes and waved, wishing he were already there. She hadn't realized, not until just that moment, how much she'd dreaded spending the evening alone. And yet, there was no one she wanted to spend it with but him. He'd infuriate her before it was over, she was certain. She was looking forward to it.

He cut back the motor so that it was a grumble instead of a roar, then guided the boat alongside the pier. When the engine shut off completely, silence snapped back—water lapping and wind in high grass.

"When are you going to take me for a ride?" Gennie demanded when he tossed her a line.

Grant stepped lightly onto the pier and watched as she deftly secured the boat. "Was I going to?"

"Maybe you weren't, but you are now." Straightening, she brushed her hands on the back of her jeans. "I was thinking about renting a little rowboat for the inlet, but I'd much rather go out to sea."

"A rowboat?" He grinned, trying to imagine her manning oars.

"I grew up on a river," she reminded him. "Sailing's in my blood."

"Is that so?" Idly, Grant took her hand, turning it over to examine the palm. It was smooth and soft and strong. "This doesn't look as if it's hoisted too many mainsails."

"I've done my share." For no reason other than she wanted to, Gennie locked her fingers with his. "There've always been seamen in my family. My great-great-grandfather was a...freelancer."

"A pirate." Intrigued, Grant caught the tip of her hair in his hand then twirled a lock around his finger. "I get the feeling you think more of that than the counts and dukes scattered through your family tree."

"Naturally. Almost anyone can find an aristocrat somewhere if they look hard enough. And he was a very good pirate."

"Good-hearted?"

"Successful," she corrected with a wicked smile. "He was almost sixty when he retired in New Orleans. My grandmother lives in the house he built there."

"With money plucked from hapless merchants," Grant finished, grinning again.

"The sea's a lawless place," Gennie said with a shrug. "You take your chances. You might get what you want—"now she grinned as well "—or you could get your head lopped off."

"It might be smarter to keep you land-locked," Grant murmured, then tugging on the hair he held, brought her closer.

Gennie put a hand to his chest for balance, but found her fingers straying up. His mouth was tempting, very tempting as it lowered toward hers. It would be smarter to resist, she knew, but she rose on her toes to meet it with her own.

With barely any pressure, he kept his lips on hers, as if unsure of his moves, unsure just how deeply he dared plunge this time. He could have swept her against him; she could have drawn him closer with no more than a sigh. Yet both of them kept that slight, tangible distance between them, as a barrier—or a safety hatch. It was still early enough for them to fight the current that was drawing them closer and closer to the point of no return.

They moved apart at the same moment and took a small, perceptible step back.

"I'd better light the charcoal," Gennie said after a moment.

"I didn't ask before," Grant began as they started down the pier. "But do you know how to cook one of those things?"

"My dear Mr. Campbell," Gennie said in a fluid drawl, "you appear to have several misconceptions about southern women. I can cook on a hot rock."

"And wash shirts in a fast stream."

"Every bit as well as you could," Gennie tossed back. "You might have some advantage on me in mechanical areas, but I'd say we're about even otherwise."

"A strike for the woman's movement?"

Gennie narrowed her eyes. "Are you about to say something snide and unintelligent?"

"No." Picking up the can of starter fluid, he handed it to her. "As a sex, you've had a legitimate gripe for several hundred years which has been handled one way as a group and another individually. Unfortunately there's still a number of doors that have to be battered down by women as a whole while the individual woman occasionally unlocks one with hardly a sound. Ever hear of Winnie Winkle?''

Fascinated despite herself, Gennie simply stared at him. ''As in Wee Willie?''

Grant laughed and leaned against the side of the barbecue. ''No. *Winnie Winkle, the Breadwinner*, a cartoon strip from the twenties. It touched on women's liberation several decades before it became a household word. Got a match?''

''Hmmm.'' Gennie dug in her pocket. ''Wasn't that a bit before your time?''

''I did some research on—social commentary in college.''

''Really?'' Again, she sensed a grain of truth that only hinted at the whole. Gennie lit the soaked charcoal, then stepped back as the fire caught and flames rose. ''Where did you go?''

Grant caught the first whiff, a summer smell he associated with his childhood. ''Georgetown.''

''They've an excellent art department there,'' Gennie said thoughtfully.

''Yeah.''

''You did study art there?'' Gennie persisted.

Grant watched the smoke rise and the haze of heat that rippled the air. ''Why?''

''Because it's obvious from that wicked little caricature you drew of me that you have talent, and that you've had training. What are you doing with it?''

''With what?''

Gennie drew her brows together in frustration. "The talent and the training. I'd have heard of you if you were painting."

"I'm not," he said simply.

"Then what are you doing?"

"What I want. Weren't you going to make a salad?"

"Damn it, Grant—"

"All right, don't get testy. I'll make it."

As he started toward the back door, Gennie swore again and grabbed his arm. "I don't understand you."

He lifted a brow. "I didn't ask you to." He saw the frustration again, but more, he saw hurt, quickly concealed. Why should he suddenly feel the urge to apologize for his need for privacy? "Gennie, let me tell you something." In an uncharacteristic gesture, he stroked his knuckles gently over her cheek. "I wouldn't be here right now if I could stay away from you. Is that enough for you?"

She wanted to say yes—and no. If she hadn't been afraid of what the words might trigger, she would have told him she was already over her head and sinking fast. Love, or perhaps the first stirrings of love that she had felt only a short time before, was growing swiftly. Instead, she smiled and slipped her hands into his.

"I'll make the salad."

It was as simple as she'd told herself it could be. In the kitchen they tossed together the dewy fresh greens and argued over the science of salad making. Meat smoked and sizzled on the grill while they sat on the grass and enjoyed the last light of the afternoon of one of the last days of summer.

Lazy smells…wet weeds, cook smoke. A few words, an easy silence. Gennie bound them up and held them close, knowing they'd be important to her on some rainy day when she was crowded by pressures and responsibilities. For now, she felt as she had when she'd been a girl and August had a few precious days left and school was light-years away. Summer always seemed to have more magic near its end.

Enough magic, Gennie mused, to make her fall in love where there was no rhyme or reason.

"What're you thinking?" Grant asked her.

She smiled and stretched her head back to the sky one last time. "That I'd better tend to that steak."

He grabbed her arm, toppling her onto her back before she could rise. "Uh-uh."

"You like it burnt?"

"Uh-uh, that's not what you were thinking," he corrected. He traced a finger over her lips, and though the gesture was absent, Gennie felt the touch in every pore.

"I was thinking about summer," she said softly. "And that it always seems to end before you're finished with it."

When she lifted her hand to his cheek, he took her wrist and held it there. "The best things always do."

As he stared down at her she smiled in that slow, easy way she had that sent ripples of need, flurries of emotion through him. All thought fled as he lowered his mouth to hers. Soft, warm, ripe, her lips answered his, then drew and drew until everything he was, felt, wished for, was focused there. Bewitched, beguiled, bedazed, he went deeper, no longer sure what path he was on, only that she was with him.

He could smell the grass beneath them, sweet and dry; a scent of summer like the smoke that curled above their heads. He wanted to touch her, every inch of that slimly rounded body that had tormented his dreams since the first moment he'd seen her. If he did once, Grant knew his dreams would never be peaceful again. If her taste alone—wild fruit, warm honey— could so easily take over his mind, what would the feel of her do to him?

His need for her was like summer—or so he told himself. It had to end before he was finished.

Lifting his head he looked down to see her eyes, faintly slanted, barely open. Without guards, she'd bring him to his knees with a look. Cautiously, he drew away then pulled her to her feet.

"We'd better get that steak off before we have to make do with salad."

Her knees were weak. Gennie would have sworn such things happened only in fiction, yet here she was throbbingly alive with joints that felt like water. Turning, she stabbed the steak with a kitchen fork to lift it to the platter.

"The fat's in the fire," she murmured.

"I was thinking the same thing myself," Grant said quietly before they walked back into the house.

By unspoken agreement, they kept the conversation light as they ate. Whatever each had felt during that short, enervating kiss was carefully stored away.

I'm not looking for a relationship, their minds rationalized separately.

We're not suited to each other in the first place.... There isn't time for this.

Good God, I'm not *falling in love.*

Shaken, Gennie lifted her wine and drank deeply while Grant scowled down at his plate.

"How's your steak?" she asked him for lack of anything else.

"What? Oh, it's good." Pushing away the uncomfortable feeling, Grant began to eat with more enthusiasm. "You cook almost as well as you paint," he decided. "Where'd you learn?"

Gennie lifted a brow. "Why, at my mammy's knee."

He grinned at the exaggerated drawl. "You've got a smart mouth, Genviève." Lifting the bottle, he poured more wine into the sturdy water glasses she'd bought in town. "I was thinking it odd that a woman who grew up with a house full of servants could grill a steak." He grinned, thinking of Shelby, who'd considered cooking a last resort.

"In the first place," she told him, "cookouts were always considered a family affair. And in the second, when you live alone you learn, or you live in restaurants."

He couldn't resist poking at her a bit as he sat back with his wine. "You've been photographed in or around every restaurant in the free world."

Not to be baited, Gennie mirrored his pose, watching him over the rim as she drank. "Is that why you get a dozen newspapers? So you can read how people live while you hibernate?"

Grant thought about it a moment. "Yeah." He didn't suppose he could have put it better himself.

"Don't you consider that an arrogant sort of attitude?"

Again he pondered on it, studying the dark red wine in his water glass. "Yeah."

Gennie laughed despite herself. "Grant, why don't you like people?"

Surprised, he looked back at her. "I do, individually in some cases, and as a whole. I just don't want them crowding me."

He meant it, she realized as she rose to stack the plates. There was just no understanding him. "Don't you ever have the need to rub elbows? Listen to a babble of voices?"

He'd had his share of elbows and voices before he'd been seventeen, Grant thought ruefully. But... No, he supposed it wasn't quite true. There were times he needed a heavy dose of humanity with all its flaws and complications; for his work and for himself. He thought of his week with the MacGregors. He'd needed that, and them, though he hadn't fully realized it until he'd settled back into his own routine.

"I have my moments," he murmured. He automatically began to clear the table as Gennie ran hot water in the sink. "No dessert?"

She looked over her shoulder to see that he was perfectly serious. He packed away food like a truck driver, yet there wasn't an ounce of spare flesh on him. Nervous energy? Metabolism? With a shake of her head, Gennie wondered why she persisted in trying to understand him. "I have a couple of fudge bars in the freezer."

Grant grinned and took her at her word. "Want one?" he asked as he ripped the thin white paper from the ice cream stick.

"No. Are you eating that because you want it or because it gets you out of drying these?" She stacked a plate into the drainer.

"Works both ways."

Leaning on the counter, he nibbled on the bar. "I could eat a carton of these when I was a kid."

Gennie rinsed another plate. "And now?"

Grant took a generous bite. "You only have two."

"A polite man would share."

"Yeah." He took another bite.

With a laugh, Gennie flicked some water into his face. "Come on, be a sport."

He held out the bar, pausing a half inch in front of her lips. Up to her elbows in soapy water, Gennie opened her mouth. Grant drew the bar away, just out of reach. "Don't get greedy," he warned.

Sending him an offended look, Gennie leaned forward enough to nibble delicately on the chocolate, then still watching him took a bite large enough to chill her mouth.

"Nasty," Grant decided, frowning at what was left of his fudge bar as Gennie laughed.

"You can have the other one," she said kindly after she'd swallowed and then dried her hands. "I just don't have any willpower when someone puts chocolate under my nose."

Deliberately, Grant ran his tongue over the bar. "Any other...weaknesses?"

As the heat expanded in her stomach, she wandered toward the porch door. "A few." She sighed as the call of swallows announced dusk. "The days are getting shorter," she murmured.

Already the lowering sun had the white clouds edged with pink and gold. The smoke from the grill struggled skyward, thinning. Near the bank of the inlet was a scrawny bush, its sparse leaves hinting of autumn red.

When Grant's hands came to her shoulders, she leaned back toward him instinctively. Together, in silence, they watched the approach of evening.

He couldn't remember the last time he'd shared a sunset with anyone, when he'd felt the desire to. Now it seemed so simple, so frighteningly simple. Would he think of her now whenever he watched the approach of evening?

"Tell me about your favorite summer," he asked abruptly.

She remembered a summer spent in the south of France and another on her father's yacht in the Aegean. Smiling, she watched the clouds deepen to rose. "I stayed with my grandmother for two weeks once while my parents had a second honeymoon in Venice. Long, lazy days with bees humming around honeysuckle blossoms. There was a big old oak outside my bedroom window just dripping with moss. Some nights I'd climb out the window to sit on a branch and look at the stars. I must have been twelve," she remembered. "There was a boy down at the stables." She laughed suddenly with her back comfortably nestled against Grant's chest. "Oh, Lord, he was a bit like Will, all sharp, awkward edges."

"You were crazy about him."

"I'd spend hours mucking out stalls and grooming horses just to get a glimpse of him. I wrote pages and pages about him in my diary and one very mushy poem."

"And kept it under your pillow."

"Apparently you've had a nodding acquaintance with twelve-year-old girls."

He thought of Shelby and grinned, resting his chin on the top of her head. Her hair smelled as though she'd washed it with rain-drenched wildflowers. "How long did it take you to get him to kiss you?"

She laughed. "Ten days. I thought I'd discovered the answer to the mysteries of the universe. I was a woman."

"No female's more sure of that than a twelve-year-old."

She smiled into the dimming sky. "More than a nodding acquaintance it appears," she commented. "One afternoon I found Angela giggling over my diary and chased her all over the house. She was..." Gennie stiffened as the grief washed over her, wave after tumultuous wave. Before Grant could tighten his hold, she had moved away from him to stare through the patched screen into twilight. "She was ten," Gennie continued in a whisper. "I threatened to shave her head if she breathed a word about what was in that diary."

"Gennie."

She shook her head as she felt his hand brush through her hair. "It'll be dark soon. You can already hear the crickets. You should start back."

He couldn't bear to hear the tears in her voice. It would be easier to leave her now, just back away. He told himself he had no skill when it came to comforting. His hands massaged gently on her shoulders. "There's a light on the boat. Let's sit down." Ignoring her resistance, Grant drew her to the porch glider. "My grandmother had one of these," he said conversationally as he slipped an arm around her and set it into creaking motion. "She had a little place on Maryland's Eastern Shore. A quiet little spot with land so flat it looked like it'd been laid out with a ruler. Ever been to the Chesapeake?"

"No." Deliberately, Gennie relaxed and closed her eyes. The motion was easy, his voice curiously soothing. She hadn't known he could speak in such quiet, gentle tones.

"Soft-shell crabs and fields of tobacco." Already he could feel the tautness in her shoulders easing. "We had to take a ferry to get to her house. It wasn't much different than this cottage except it was two stories. My father and I could go across the street and fish. I caught a trout once using a piece of Longhorn cheese as bait."

Grant continued to talk, ramble really, recounting things he'd forgotten, things he'd never spoken of aloud before. Unimportant things that droned quietly on the air while the light softened. For the moment it seemed to be the right thing, the thing she needed. He wasn't certain he had anything else to give.

He kept the motion of the glider going while her head rested against his shoulder and wondered how he'd never noticed just how peaceful dusk could be when you shared it with someone.

Gennie sighed, listening more to his tone than his words. She let herself drift as the chirp of crickets grew more insistent.... Dreams are often no more than memories.

"Oh, Gennie, you should have been there!" Angela, golden and vibrant, turned in her seat to laugh while Gennie maneuvered through the traffic of downtown New Orleans. The streets were damp with a chilly February rain, but nothing could dampen Angela. She was sunlight and spring flowers.

"I'd rather have been there than freezing in New York," Gennie returned.

"You can't freeze when you're basking in the lime-light," Angela countered, twisting a bit closer to her sister.

"Wanna bet?"

"You wouldn't have missed that showing for a dozen parties."

No, she wouldn't have, Gennie thought with a smile. But Angela... "Tell me about it."

"It was so much fun! All that noise and music. It was so crowded, you couldn't take a step without bumping into someone. The next time Cousin Frank throws a bash on his houseboat you have to come."

Gennie sent Angela a quick grin. "It doesn't sound like I was missed."

Angela laughed, the quick bubble that was irresistible. "Well, I got a little tired of answering questions about my talented sister."

Gennie gave a snort as she stopped at a light. She could see the hazy red glow as the windshield wipers moved briskly back and forth. "They just use that as a line to get to you."

"Well, there was someone..." When Angela trailed off, Gennie turned to look at her. So beautiful, she thought. Gold and cream with eyes almost painfully alive and vivid.

"Someone?"

"Oh, Gennie." Excitement brought a soft pink to her cheeks. "He's gorgeous. I could hardly make a coherent sentence when he started to talk to me."

"You?"

"Me," Angela agreed, laughing again. "It felt like someone had drained off half my brain. And now... Well, I've been seeing him all week. I think—ta-da—this is it."

"After a week?" Gennie countered.

"After five seconds. Oh, Gennie, don't be practical. I'm in love. You have to meet him."

Gennie shifted into first as she waited for the light to change. "Do I get to size him up?"

Angela shook back her rich gold hair and laughed as the light turned green. "Oh, I feel wonderful, Gennie. Absolutely wonderful!"

The laugh was the last thing Gennie heard before the squeal of brakes. She saw the car skidding toward them through the intersection. In the dream it was always so slow, second by terrifying second, closer and closer. Water spewed out from the tires and seemed to hang in the air.

There wasn't time to breathe, there wasn't time to react or prevent before there was the sound of metal striking metal, the explosion of blinding lights. Terror. Pain. And darkness.

"No!" She jerked upright, rigid with fear and shock. There were arms around her, holding her close...safe. Crickets? Where had they come from? The light, the car. Angela.

Gasping for breath, Gennie stared out at the darkened inlet while Grant's voice murmured something comforting in her ear.

"I'm sorry." Pushing away, she rose, lifting nervous hands to her hair. "I must have dozed off. Poor company," she continued in a jerky voice. "You should have given me a jab, and—"

"Gennie." He stood, grabbing her arm. "Stop it."

She crumbled. He hadn't expected such complete submission and had no defense against it. "Don't," he murmured, stroking her hair as she clung to him. "Gennie, don't cry. It's all right now."

"Oh, God, it hasn't happened in weeks." She buried her face against his chest as the grief washed over her as fresh as the first hour. "At first, right after the accident, I'd go through it every time I closed my eyes."

"Come on." He kissed the top of her head. "Sit down."

"No, I can't—I need to walk." She held him tight another moment, as if gathering her strength. "Can we walk?"

"Sure." Bringing her to his side, Grant opened the screen door. For a time he was silent, his arm around her shoulders as they skirted the inlet and walked aimlessly. But he knew he needed to hear as much as she needed to tell. "Gennie, talk to me."

"I was remembering the accident," she said slowly, but her voice was calmer now. "Sometimes when I'd dream of it, I'd be quick enough, swerve out of the way of that car and everything was so different. Then I'd wake up and nothing was different at all."

"It's a natural reaction," he told her, though the thought of her being plagued by nightmares began to gnaw at his gut. He'd lived through a few of his own. "They'll fade after a while."

"I know. It hardly ever happens anymore." She let out a long breath and seemed steadier for it. "When it does, it's so clear. I can see the rain splattering on the windshield right before the wipers whisk it away. There're puddles near the curbs, and Angela's voice is so—vital. She was so beautiful, Grant, not just her face, but her. She never outgrew sweetness. She was telling me about a party she'd been to where she'd met someone. She was in love, bubbling over with it. The last thing she said was that she felt wonderful, absolutely wonderful. Then I killed her."

Grant took her shoulders, shaking her hard. "What the hell kind of craziness is that?"

"It was my fault," Gennie returned with deadly calm. "If I'd seen that car, if I'd seen it just seconds earlier. Or if I'd *done* something, hit the brakes, the gas, anything. The impact was all on her side. I had a mild concussion, a few bruises, and she..."

"Would you feel better if you'd been seriously injured?" he demanded roughly. "You can mourn for her, cry for her, but you can't take the blame."

"I was driving, Grant. How do I forget that?"

"You don't forget it," he snapped back, unnerved by the dull pain in her voice. "But you put it in perspective. There was nothing you could have done, you know that."

"You don't understand." She swallowed because the tears were coming and she'd thought she was through with them. "I loved her so much. She was part of me—a part of me I needed very badly. When you lose someone who was vital to your life, it takes a chunk out of you."

He did understand—the pain, the need to place blame. Gennie blamed herself for exposing her sister to death. Grant blamed his father for exposing himself. Neither way changed the loss. "Then you have to live without that chunk."

"You can't know what it's like," she began.

"My father was killed when I was seventeen," he said, saying the words he would rather have avoided. "I needed him."

Gennie let her head fall against his chest. She didn't offer sympathy, knowing he wanted none. "What did you do?"

"Hated—for a long time. That was easy." Without realizing it, he was holding her against him again, gaining comfort as well as giving it. "Accepting's tougher. Everyone does it in different ways."

"How did you?"

"By realizing there was nothing I could have done to stop it." Drawing her away a little, he lifted her chin with his hand. "Just as there was nothing you could have done."

"It's easier, isn't it, to tell yourself you could have done something than to admit you were helpless?"

He'd never thought about it—perhaps refused to think about it. "Yeah."

"Thank you. I know you didn't want to tell me that even more than I didn't want to tell you. We can get very selfish with our grief—and our guilt."

He brushed the hair away from her temples. He kissed her cheeks where tears were still drying and felt a surge of tenderness that left him shaken. Defenseless, she made him vulnerable. If he kissed her now, really kissed her, she'd have complete power over him. With more effort than he'd realized it would take, Grant drew away from her.

"I have to get back," he said, deliberately putting his hands in his pockets. "Will you be all right?"

"Yes, but—I'd like you to stay." The words were out before she realized she'd thought them. But she wouldn't take them back. Something flared in his eyes. Even in the dim light she saw it. Desire, need, and something quickly banked and shuttered.

"Not tonight."

The tone had her brows drawing together in puzzlement. "Grant," she began, and reached for him.

"Not tonight," he repeated, stopping the motion of her outstretched hand.

Gennie put it behind her back as if he'd slapped it. "All right." Her pride surged forward to cover the hurt of fresh rejection. "I appreciated the company." Turning, she started back to the house.

Grant watched her go, then swore, taking a step after her. "Gennie."

"Good night, Grant." The screen door swung shut behind her.

Chapter Seven

She was going to lose it. Gennie cast a furious look at the clouds whipping in from the north, and swore. Damn, she was going to lose the light and she wasn't ready. The energy was pouring through her, flowing from her mind and heart to her hand in one of the rare moments an artist recognizes as *right*. Everything, everything told her that something lasting, something important would spring onto the canvas that morning; she had only to let herself go with it. But to go with it now, she had to race against the storm.

Gennie knew she had perhaps thirty minutes before the clouds would spoil her light, an hour before the rain closed out everything. Already a distant thunder rumbled over the sound of crashing waves. She cast a defiant look at the sky. By God, she would beat it yet!

The impetus was with her, an urgency that said to-day—it's going to happen today. Whatever she'd done before—the sketches, the preliminary work, the spread of paint on canvas—was just a preparation for what she would create today.

Excitement rippled across her skin with the wind. And a frustration. She seemed to need them both to draw from. Maybe a storm was brewing in her as well. It had seemed so since the night before when her mood had fluctuated and twisted, with Grant, without him. The last rejection had left her numb, ominously calm. Now her emotions were raging free again—fury, passion, pride, and torment. Gennie could pour them into her art, liberating them so that they wouldn't fester inside her.

Need him? No, she needed neither him nor anyone, she told herself as she streaked her brush over the canvas. Her work was enough to fill her life, cleanse her wounds. It was always fresh, always constant. As long as her eyes could see and her fingers could lift pencil or brush, it would be with her.

It had been her friend during her childhood, a solace during the pangs of adolescence. It was as demanding as a lover, and as greedy for her passion. And it was passion she felt now, a vibrant, physical passion that drove her forward. The moment was ripe, and the electricity in the air only added to the sense of urgency that shimmered inside her.

Now! it shouted at her. The time for merging, soul and heart and mind was now. If not now, it would be never. The clouds raced closer. She vowed to beat them.

Skin cool with anticipation, blood hot, Grant came outside. Like a wolf, he'd scented something in the air and had come in search of it. He'd been too restless to work, to tense too relax. Something had been driving at him all morning, urging him to move, to look, to find. He'd told himself it was the approach of the storm, the lack of sleep. But he'd known, without understanding, that each of those things was only a part of the whole. Something was brewing, brewing in more than that cauldron of a sky.

He was hungry without wanting to eat, dissatisfied without knowing what he would change. Restless, reckless, he'd fretted against the confines of his studio all walls and glass. Instinct had led him out to seek the wind and the sea. And Gennie.

He'd known she'd be there, though he'd been convinced that he'd closed his mind to even the thought of her. But now, seeing her, he was struck, just as surely as the north sky was struck with the first silver thread of lightning.

He'd never seen her like this, but he'd known. She stood with her head thrown back in abandon to her work, her eyes glowing green with power. There was a wildness about her only partially due to the wind that swept up her hair and billowed the thin smock she wore. There was strength in the hand that guided the brush so fluidly and yet with such purpose. She might have been a queen overlooking her dominion. She might have been a woman waiting for a lover. As his blood quickened with need, Grant thought she was both.

Where was the woman who'd wept in his arms only hours before? Where was the fragility, the defenselessness that had terrified him? He'd given her what comfort he could, though he knew little of soothing tearful women. He'd spoken of things he hadn't said aloud in fifteen years—because she'd needed to hear them and he, for some indefinable reason, had needed to say them. And he'd left her because he'd felt himself being sucked into something unknown, and inevitable.

Now, she looked invulnerable, magnificent. This was a woman no man would ever resist, a woman who could choose and discard lovers with a single gesture. It wasn't fear he felt now, but challenge, and with the challenge a desire so huge it threatened to swallow him.

She stopped painting on a roll of thunder then looked up to the sky in a kind of exaltation. He heard her laugh, once, with an arousing defiance that had him struggling with a fresh slap of desire.

Who in God's name was she? he demanded. And why, in heaven and hell, couldn't he stay away?

The excitement that had driven her to finish the painting lingered. It was done, Gennie thought with a breathless triumph. And yet...there was something more. Her passion hadn't been diffused by the consummation of woman and art, but spun in her still; restless, waiting.

Then she saw him, with the sea and the storm at his back. The wind blew wilder. Her blood pounded with it. For a long moment they only stared at each other while thunder and lightning inched closer.

Ignoring him, and the flash of heat that demanded she close the distance between them, Gennie turned back to the canvas. This and only this was what called to her, she told herself. This and only this was what she needed.

Grant watched her pack her paints and brushes. There was something both regal and defiant about the way she had turned her back on him and gone about her business. Yet there was no denying that jolt of recognition he had felt when their gazes had locked. Under his feet the ground shook with the next roll of thunder. He went to her.

The light shifted, dimming as clouds rolled over the sun. The air was so charged, sparks could be felt along the skin. Gennie packed up her gear with deft, steady hands. She'd beaten the storm that morning. She could beat anything.

"Geneviève." She wasn't Gennie now. He'd seen Gennie in the churchyard, laughing with young, fresh delight. It had been Gennie who had clung to him, weeping. This woman's laugh would be low and seductive, and she would shed no tears at all. Whichever, whoever she was, Grant was drawn to her, irrevocably.

"Grant." Gennie closed the lid on her paint case before she turned. "You're out early."

"You've finished."

"Yes." The wind blew his hair wildly around his face, and while the face was set, his eyes were dark and restless. Gennie knew her own emotions matched his like two halves of the same coin. "I've finished."

"You'll go now." He could see the flush of triumph on her face and the moody, unpredictable green of her eyes.

"From here?" She tossed her head as her gaze shifted to the sea. The waves were swelling higher, and no boat dared test them now. "Yes. I have other things I want to paint."

It was what he wanted. Hadn't he wanted to be rid of her from the very first? But Grant said nothing as the grumbling thunder rolled closer.

"You'll have your solitude back." Gennie's smile was light and mocking. "That's what's most important to you, isn't it? And I've gotten what I needed here.''

His eyes narrowed, but he wasn't certain of the origin of his temper. "Have you?"

"Have a look," she invited with a gesture of her hand.

He hadn't wanted to see the painting, had deliberately avoided even a glance at it. Now her eyes dared him and the flick of her wrist was too insolent to deny. Hooking his thumbs in his pockets, Grant turned toward the canvas.

She saw too much of what he needed there, what he felt. The power of limitless sea, the glory of space and unending challenge. She'd scorned muted colors and had chosen bold. She'd forsaken delicacy for muscle. What had been a blank canvas was now as full of force as the turbulent Atlantic, and as full of secrets. The secrets there were nature's, as the strength and solidity of the lighthouse were man's. She'd captured both, pitting them against each other even while showing their timeless harmony.

The painting moved him, disturbed him, pulled at him, as much as its creator.

Gennie felt the tension build up at the base of her neck as Grant only frowned at the painting. She knew it was everything she'd wanted it to be, felt it was perhaps the best work she'd ever done. But it was his—his world, his force, his secrets that had dominated the emotions she'd felt when she'd painted it. Even as she'd finished, the painting had stopped being hers and had become his.

Grant took a step away from the painting and looked out to sea. The lightning was closer; he saw it shimmer dangerously behind the dark, angry clouds.

He seemed to have lost the words, the phrases that had always come so easily to him. He couldn't think of anything but her, and the need that had risen up to work knots in his stomach. "It's fine," he said flatly.

He could have struck her and hurt her no less. Her small gasp was covered by the moan of the wind. For a moment Gennie stared at his back while pain rocketed through her. Rejection...would she never stop setting herself up for his rejection?

Pain altered to anger in the space of seconds. She didn't need his approval, his pleasure, his understanding. She had everything she needed within herself. In raging silence she slipped the canvas into its carrying case, then folded her easel. Gathering her things together, she turned toward him slowly.

"Before I go, I'd like to tell you something." Her voice was cool over flowing vowels. "It isn't often one finds one's first impression was so killingly accurate. The first night I met you, I thought you were a rude, arrogant man with no redeeming qualities." The wind blew her hair across her eyes and with a toss of her head she sent it flying back so that she could keep her icy gaze on his. "It's very gratifying to learn just how right I was...and to be able to dislike you so intensely." Chin high, Gennie turned and walked to her car.

She jerked up the trunk of her car and put her equipment and canvas in, perversely glad to flow with the fury that consumed her. When Grant's hand closed over her arm, she slammed the trunk closed and whirled around, ready to battle on any terms, any grounds. Blind with her own emotions, she didn't notice the heat in his eyes or the raggedness of his breathing.

"Do you think I'm just going to let you walk away?" he demanded. "Do you think you can walk into my life and take and not leave anything behind?"

Her chest was heaving, her eyes brilliant. With calculated disdain, she looked down at the fingers that circled her arm. "Take your hand off me," she told him, spacing her words with insolent precision.

Lightning shot across the sky as they stared at each other, cold white heat against boiling gray and angry purple. The deafening roar of thunder drowned out Grant's oath. The moment stood poised, crackling, then swirled like the wind that screamed in triumph.

"You should have taken my advice," he said between his teeth, "and stuck with your counts and barons." Then he was pulling her across the tough grass, against the wind.

"What the hell do you think you're doing?"

"What I should have done the minute you barged into my life."

Murder? Gennie stared at the cliffs and the raging sea below. God knew he looked ready for it at that moment—and perhaps he would have liked her to believe he was capable of tossing her over the edge. But she knew what the violence in him meant, where it would lead them both. She fought him wildly as he pulled her toward the lighthouse.

"You must be mad! Let me go!"

"I must be," he agreed tightly. Lightning forked again, opening the sky. Rain spewed out.

"I said take your hands off me!"

He whirled to her then, his face sculptured and shadowed in the crazed light of the storm. "It's too late for that!" he shouted at her. "Damn it, you know it as well as I do. It was too late from the first minute." Rain poured over them, pounding and warm.

"I won't be dragged into your bed, do you hear me!" She grabbed his soaking shirt with her free hand while her body vibrated with fury and with wanting. "I won't be dragged anywhere. Do you think you can just suddenly decide you need a lover and haul me off?"

His breath was raging in and out of his lungs. The rain pouring down his face only accented the passionate darkness of his eyes. She was sleek and wet. A siren? Maybe she was, but he'd already wrecked on the reef. "Not any lover." He swung her against him so that their wet clothes fused then seemed to melt away. "You. Damn it, Gennie, you know it's you."

Their faces were close, their eyes locked. Each had forgotten the storm around them as the tempest within took over. Heart pounded against heart. Need pounded against need. Full of fear and triumph, she threw her head back.

"Show me."

Grant crushed her closer so that not even the wind could have forced its way between. "Here," he said roughly. "By God, here and now."

His mouth took hers madly, and she answered. Unleashed, the passion drove them far past sanity, beyond the civilized and into the dark tunnel of chaotic desire. His lips sped across her face, seeking to devour all that could be consumed and more. When his teeth scraped over the cord of her neck, Gennie moaned and drew him with her to the ground.

Raw, keening wind, hard, driving rain, the pound and crash of the stormy sea. They were nothing in the face of this tempest. Grant forgot them as he pressed against her, feeling every line and curve as though he'd already torn the clothes from her. Her heart pounded. It seemed as if it had worked its way inside his chest to merge with his.

Her body felt like a furnace. He hadn't known there could be such heat from a living thing. But alive she was, moving under him, hands seeking, mouth greedy. The rain sluicing over them should have cooled the fire, yet it stoked it higher so that the water might have sizzled on contact.

He knew only greed, only ageless need and primitive urges. She'd bewitched him from the first instant, and now, at last, he succumbed. Her hands were in his hair, bringing his mouth back to hers again and again so that her lips could leave him breathless, arouse more hunger.

They rolled on the wet grass until she was on top of him, her mouth ravaging his with a strength and power only he could match. In a frenzy, she dragged at his shirt, yanking and tugging until it was over his head and discarded. With a long, low moan she ran her hands over him. Grant's reason shattered.

Roughly, he pushed her on her back, cutting off her breath as lightning burst overhead. Ignoring buttons, he pulled the blouse from her, desperate to touch what he had denied himself for days. His hands slid over her wet skin, kneading, possessing, hurrying in his greed for more. And when she arched against him, agile and demanding, he buried his mouth at her breast and lost himself.

He tasted the rain on her, laced with summer thunder and her own night scent. Like a drowning man he clung to her as he sank beneath the depths. He knew what it was to want a woman, but not like this. Desire could be controlled, channeled, guided. So what was it that pounded in him? His fingers bruised her, but he was unaware in his desperation to take all and take it quickly.

When he dragged the jeans down her hips, he felt both arousal and frustration as they clung to her skin and those smooth, narrow curves. Struggling with the wet denim, he followed its inching progress with his mouth, thrilling as Gennie arched and moaned. His teeth scraped over her hip, down her thigh to the inside of her knee as he pulled the jeans down her, then left them in a heap.

Mindlessly, he plunged his tongue into her and heard her cry out with the wind. Heat suffused him. Rain fell on his back unfelt, ran from his hair onto her skin but did nothing to wash away the passion that drove them both closer and closer to the peak.

Then they were both fighting with his jeans, hands tangling together while their lips fused again. The sounds coming low from her throat might have been his name or some new spell she was weaving over him. He no longer cared.

Lightning illuminated her face once, brilliantly—the slash of cheekbone, the eyes slanted and nearly closed, the soft full lips parted and trembling with her breathing. At that moment she was witch, and he, willingly bewitched.

With his mouth against the hammering pulse in her throat, he plunged into her, taking her with a violent kind of worship he didn't understand. When she stiffened and cried out, Grant struggled to find both his sanity and the reason. Then she was wrapped around him drawing him into the satin-coated darkness.

Breathless, dazed, empty, Grant lay with his face buried in Gennie's hair. The rain still fell, but until that moment he didn't realize that it had lost its force. The storm was passed, consumed by itself like all things of passion. He felt the hammer-trip beat of her heart beneath him, and her trembles. Shutting his eyes, he tried to gather his strength and the control that meant lucidity.

"Oh, God." His voice was rough and raw. The apology wouldn't come; he thought it less than useless. "Why didn't you tell me?" he murmured as he rolled from her to lie on his back against the wet grass. "Damn it, Gennie, why didn't you tell me?"

She kept her eyes closed so that the rain fell on her lids, over her face and throbbing body. Was this how it was supposed to be? she wondered. Should she feel so spent, so enervated while her skin hummed everywhere, everywhere his had touched it? Should she feel as though every lock she had, had been broken? By whom, him or her, it didn't matter. But her privacy was gone, and the need for it. Yet now, hearing the harsh question—accusation?—she felt a ripple of pain sharper than the loss of innocence. She said nothing.

"Gennie, you let me think you were—"

"What?" she demanded, opening her eyes. The clouds were still dark, she saw, but the lightning was gone.

Cursing himself, Grant dragged a hand through his hair. "Gennie, you should have told me you hadn't been with a man before." And how was it possible, he wondered, that she'd let no man touch her before? That he was the first...the only.

"Why?" she said flatly, wishing he would go, wishing she had the strength to leave. "It was my business."

Swearing, he shifted, leaning over her. His eyes were dark and angry, but when she tried to pull away, he pinned her. "I don't have much gentleness," he told her, and the words were unsteady with feeling. "But I would have used all I had, I would have tried to find more, for you." When she only stared at him, Grant lowered his forehead to hers. "Gennie..."

Her doubts, her fears, melted at that one softly murmured word. "I wasn't looking for gentleness then," she whispered. Framing his face with her hands, she lifted it. "But now..." She smiled, and watched the frown fade from his eyes.

He dropped a kiss on her lips, soft, more like a whisper, then rising, lifted her into his arms. Gennie laughed at the feeling of weightlessness and ease. "What're you doing now?"

"Taking you inside so you can warm up, dry off, and make love with me again—maybe not in that order."

Gennie curled her arms around his neck. "I'm beginning to like your ideas. What about our clothes?"

"We can salvage what's left of them later." He pushed open the door of the lighthouse. "We won't be needing them for quite a while."

"Definitely liking your ideas." She pressed her mouth against his throat. "Are you really going to carry me up those stairs?"

"Yeah."

Gennie cast a look at the winding staircase and tightened her hold. "I'd just like to mention it wouldn't be terribly romantic if you were to trip and drop me."

"The woman casts aspersions on my machismo."

"On your balance," she corrected as he started up. She shivered as her wet skin began to chill, then abruptly laughed. "Grant, did it occur to you what those assorted piles of clothes would look like if someone happened by?"

"They'd probably look a great deal like what they are," he considered. "And it should discourage anyone from trespassing. I should have thought of it before—much better than a killer-dog sign."

She sighed, partially from relief as they reached the landing. "You're hopeless. Anyone would think you were Clark Kent."

Grant stopped in the doorway to the bathroom to stare at her. "Come again?"

"You know, concealing a secret identity. Though you're anything but mild-mannered," she added as she toyed with a damp curl that hung over his ear. "You've set up this lighthouse as some kind of Fortress of Solitude."

The long intense look continued. "What was Clark Kent's Earth mother's name?"

"Is this a quiz?"

"Do you know?"

She arched a brow because his eyes were so suddenly serious. "Martha."

"I'll be damned," he murmured. He laughed, then gave her a quick kiss that was puzzlingly friendly considering they were naked and pressed together. "You continue to surprise me, Geneviève. I think I'm crazy about you."

The light words went straight to her heart and turned it over. "Because I know Superman's adoptive mother's first name?"

Grant nuzzled his cheek against her, the first wholly sweet gesture she'd ever seen in him. In that one instant she was lost, as she'd never been lost before. "For one thing." Feeling her tremble, Grant drew her closer. "Come on, into the shower; you're freezing."

He stepped into the tub before he set her down, then still holding her close, pressed his mouth to hers in a long, lingering kiss. With the storm, with the passion, she'd felt invulnerable. Now, no longer innocent, no longer unaware, the nerves returned. Only a short time before she had given herself to him, perhaps demanded that he take her, but now she could only cling while her mind reeled with the wonder of it.

When the water came on full and hot, she jolted, gasping. With a low laugh, Grant stroked a hand intimately over her hip. "Feel good?"

It did, after the initial shock, but Gennie tilted back her head and eyed him narrowly. "You might have warned me."

"Life's full of surprises."

Like falling in love, she thought, when you hadn't the least intention of doing so. Gennie smiled, finding her arms had wound around his neck.

"You know..." He traced his tongue lightly over her mouth. "I'm getting used to the taste—and the feel of you wet. It's tempting just to stay right here for the next couple of hours."

She nuzzled against him when he ran his hands down her back. Strong hands, toughened in contrast to the elegance of their shape. There were no others she could ever imagine touching her.

With the steam rising around him, and Gennie soft and giving in his arms, Grant felt that rushing, heady desire building again. His muscles contracted with it— tightening, preparing.

"No, not this time," he murmured, pressing his mouth to her throat. This time he would remember her fragility and the wonder of being the only man to ever possess her. Whatever tenderness he had, or could find in himself, would be for her.

"You should dry off." He nibbled lightly at her lips before he drew her away. She was smiling, but her eyes were uncertain. As he turned off the water he tried to ignore the very real fear her vulnerability brought to him. Taking a towel from the rack, he stroked it over her face. "Here, lift your arms."

She did, laying her hands on his shoulders as he wrapped the towel around her. Slowly, running soft, undemanding kisses over her face, he drew the towel together to knot it loosely at her breasts. Gennie closed her eyes, the better to soak up the sensation of being pampered.

Using a fresh towel, Grant began to dry her hair. Gently, lazily, while her heart began to race, he rubbed the towel over it. "Warm?" he murmured, dipping his head to nibble at her ear. "You're trembling."

How could she answer when her heart was hammering in her throat? Heat was creeping into her, yet her body shivered with anticipation, uncertainties, longings. He had only to touch his mouth to hers to know that for that moment, for always, she was his.

"I want you," he said softly. "I wanted you right from the start." He skimmed his tongue over her ear. "You knew that."

"Yes." The word came out breathlessly, like a sigh.

"Do you know how much more I want you now than I did even an hour ago?" His mouth covered hers before she could answer. "Come to bed, Gennie."

He didn't carry her, but took her hand so that they could walk together into the thin gray light of his room. Her pulses pounded. The first time there had been no thought, no doubts. Desire had ruled her and the power had flowed. Now her mind was clear and her nerves jumping. She knew now where he could take her with a touch, with a taste. The journey was as much feared as it was craved.

"Grant—"

But he barely touched her, only cupping her face as they stood beside the bed. "You're beautiful." His eyes were on hers, intense, searching. "The first time I saw you, you took my breath away. You still do."

As moved by the long look and soft words as she had been by the tempestuous kisses, she reached up to take his wrists. "I don't need the words unless you want to give them. I just want to be with you."

"Whatever I tell you will be the truth, or I won't tell you at all." He leaned toward her, touching his mouth to hers, but nibbling only, testing the softness, lingering over that honey-steeped taste. As he took her deep with tenderness, his fingers moved over her face, skimming, stroking. Gennie's head went light while her body grew heavy. She barely felt the movement when they lowered to the bed.

Then it seemed she felt everything—the tiny nubs in the bedspread, the not quite smooth, not quite rough texture of Grant's palms, the thin mat of hair on his chest. All, she felt them all, as if her skin had suddenly become as soft and sensitive as a newborn's. And he treated her as though she were that precious with the slow, whisper-light kisses he brushed over her face and the hands that touched her—arousing, but stopping just short of demand.

The floating weightlessness she had experienced in the churchyard drifted back over her, but now, with the shivering excitement of knowledge. Aware of where they could lead each other, Gennie sighed. This time the journey would be luxurious, lazy and loving.

The light through the window was thin, misty gray from the clouds that still hid the sun. It cast shadows and mysteries. She could hear the sea—not the deafening, titanic roar, but the echo and the promise of power. And when he murmured to her, it was like the sea, with its passionate pull and thrust. The urgency she had felt before had become a quiet enjoyment. Though the needs were no less, there was a comfort here, an unquestioning trust she'd never expected to feel. He would protect if she needed him, cherish in his own fashion. Beneath the demands and impatience was a man who would give unselfishly where he cared. Discovering that was discovering everything.

Touch me—don't ever stop touching me. And he seemed to hear her silent request as he caressed, lingered, explored. The pleasure was liquid and light, like a lazy river, like rain misting. Her mind was so clouded with him, only him, she no longer thought of her body as separate, but a part of the two that made one whole.

Soft murmurs and quiet sighs, the warmth that only flesh can bring to flesh. Gennie learned of him—the man he showed so rarely to anyone. Sensitivity, because it was not his way, was all the sweeter. Gentleness, so deeply submerged, was all the more arousing.

She hardly knew when her pliancy began to kindle to excitement. But he did. The subtle change in her movements, her breathing, had a shiver of pleasure darting down his spine. And he drew yet more pleasure in the mere watching of her face in the gloomy light. A flicker of passion reminded him that no one had ever touched her as he did. And no one would. For so long he'd taken such care not to allow anyone to get too close, to block off any feelings of possession, to avoid being possessed. Though the proprietary sensation disturbed him, he couldn't fight it. She was his. Grant told himself it didn't yet mean he was hers. Yet he could think of no one else.

He ran kisses over her slowly, until his mouth brushed then loitered at her shoulder. And when he felt her yield, completely, unquestioningly, he took her once, gasping, to the edge. On her moan, he pressed his lips to hers, wanting to feel the sound as well as hear it.

Mindless, boneless, burning, Gennie moved with him, responding to the agonizingly slow pace by instinct alone. She wanted to rush, she wanted to stay in that cloudy world of dreams forever. Now, and only now, did she fully understand why the coming together of two separate beings was called making love.

She opened to him, offering everything. When he slipped inside her she felt his shudder, heard the groan that was muffled against her throat. His breath rasped against her ear but he kept the pace exquisitely slow. There couldn't be so much—she'd never known there could be—but he showed her.

She drifted down a tunnel with soft melting edges. Deeper and lusher it grew until her whole existence was bound there in the velvet heat that promised forever. Reason peeled away layer by layer so that her body was guided by senses alone. He was trembling—was she? As her hands glided over his shoulders she could feel the hard, tense muscles there while his movements were gentle and easy. Through the mists of pleasure she knew he was blocking off his own needs for hers. A wave of emotion struck her that was a hundred times greater than passion.

"Grant." His name was only a whisper as her arms tightened around him. "Now. Take me now."

"Gennie." He lifted his face so that she had a glimpse of dark, dark eyes before his mouth met hers. His control seemed to snap at the contact and he swallowed her gasps as he rushed with her to the peak.

There were no more thoughts nor the need for any.

Chapter Eight

With a slow stretch and a long sigh, Gennie woke. Ingrained habit woke her early and quickly. Her first feeling of disorientation faded almost at once. No, the sun-washed window wasn't hers, but she knew whose it was. She knew where she was and why.

The morning warmth had a new texture—body to body, man to woman, lover to lover. Simultaneous surges of contentment and excitement swam through her to chase away any sense of drowsiness. Turning her head, Gennie watched Grant sleep.

He sprawled, taking up, Gennie discovered to her amusement, about three-fourths of the bed. During the night, he had nudged her to within four inches of the edge. His arm was tossed carelessly across her body—not loverlike, she thought wryly, but because she just happened to be in his space. He had most of her pillow. Against the plain white, his face was deeply tanned, shadowed by the stubble that grew on his jaw. Looking at him, Gennie realized he was completely relaxed as she had seen him only once before—on their walk along the beach.

What drives you, Grant? she wondered as she gave in to the desire to toy with the tips of his rumpled hair. What makes you so intense, so solitary? And why do I want so badly to understand and share whatever secrets you keep?

With a fingertip, carefully, delicately, Gennie traced down the line of his jaw. A strong face, she thought, almost hard, and yet occasionally, unexpectedly the humor and sensitivity would come into his eyes. Then the hardness would vanish and only the strength would remain.

Rude, remote, arrogant; he was all of those things. And she loved him—despite it, perhaps because of it. It had been the gentleness he had shown her that had allowed her to admit it, accept it, but it had been true all along.

She longed to tell him, to say those simple, exquisite words. She'd shared her body with him, given her innocence and her trust. Now she wanted to share her emotions. Love, she believed, was meant to be given freely, without conditions. Yet she knew him well enough to understand that step would have to be taken by him first. His nature demanded it. Another man might be flattered, pleased, even relieved to have a woman state her feelings so easily. Grant, Gennie reflected, would feel cornered.

Lying still, watching him, she wondered if it had been a woman who had caused him to isolate himself. Gennie felt certain it had been pain or disillusionment that had made him so determined to be unapproachable. There was a basic kindness in him which he hid, a talent he apparently wasn't using and a warmth he hoarded. Why? With a sigh, she brushed the hair from his forehead. They were his mysteries; she only hoped she had the patience to wait until he was ready to share them.

Warm, content, Gennie snuggled against him, murmuring his name. Grant's answer was an unintelligible mutter as he shifted onto his stomach and buried his face in the pillow. The movement cost Gennie a few more precious inches of mattress.

"Hey!" Laughing, she shoved against his shoulder. "Move over."

No response.

You're a romantic devil, Gennie thought wryly, then pressing her lips to that unbudgable shoulder, slipped out of the bed. Grant immediately took advantage of all the available space.

A loner, Gennie thought, studying him as he lay crosswise over the twisted sheets. He wasn't a man used to making room for anyone. With a last thoughtful glance, Gennie walked across the hall to shower.

Gradually the sound of running water woke him. Hazy, Grant lay still, sleepily debating how much effort it would take to open his eyes. It was his ingrained habit to put off the moment of waking until it could no longer be avoided.

With his face buried in the pillow, he could smell Gennie. It brought dreamy images to him, images sultry but not quite formed. There were soft, fuzzy-edged pictures that both aroused and soothed.

Barely half awake, Grant shifted enough to discover he was alone in bed. Her warmth was still there—on the sheets, on his skin. He lay steeped in it a moment, not certain why it felt so right, not trying to reason out the answers.

He remembered the feel of her, the taste, the way her pulse would leap under the touch of his finger. Had there ever been a woman who had made him want so badly? Who could make him comfortable one moment and wild the next? How close was he to the border between want and need, or had he already crossed it?

They were more questions he couldn't deal with— not now while his mind was still clouded with sleep and with Gennie. He needed to shake off the first and distance himself from the second before he could find any answers.

Groggy, Grant sat up, running a hand over his face as Gennie came back in.

"Morning." With her hair wrapped in a towel and Grant's robe belted loosely at her waist, Gennie dropped onto the edge of the bed. Linking her hands behind his neck, she leaned over and kissed him. She smelled of his soap and shampoo—something that made the easy kiss devastatingly intimate. Even as this began to soak into him, she drew away to give him a friendly smile. "Awake yet?"

"Nearly." Because he wanted to see her hair, Grant pulled the towel from her head and let it drop to the floor. "Have you been up long?"

"Only since you pushed me out of bed." She laughed when his brows drew together. "That's not much of an exaggeration. Want some coffee?"

"Yeah." As she rose, Grant took her hand, holding it until her smile became puzzled. What did he want to say to her? Grant wondered. What did he want to tell her—or himself? He wasn't certain of anything except the knowledge that whatever was happening inside him was already too far advanced to stop.

"Grant?"

"I'll be down in a minute," he mumbled, feeling foolish. "I'll fix breakfast this time."

"All right." Gennie hesitated, wondering if he would say whatever he'd really meant to say, then she left him alone.

Grant remained in bed a moment, listening to the sound of her footsteps on his stairs. Her footsteps—his stairs. Somehow, the line of demarcation was smearing. He wasn't certain he'd be able to lie in his bed again without thinking of her curled beside him.

But he'd had other women, Grant reminded himself. He'd enjoyed them, appreciated them. Forgotten them. Why was it he was so certain there was nothing about Gennie he'd forget? Nothing, down to that small, faint birthmark he'd found on her hip—a half moon he could cover with his pinky. Foolishly it had pleased him to discover it—something he knew no other man had seen or touched.

He was acting like an idiot, he told himself—enchanted by the fact that he was her first lover, obsessed with the idea of being her last, her only. He needed to be alone for a while, that was all, to put his feelings back in perspective. The last thing he wanted was to start tying strings on her, and in turn, on himself.

Rising, he rummaged in his drawers until he found a pair of cutoffs. He'd fix breakfast, send her on her way, then get back to work.

But when he reached the bottom of the stairs, he smelled the coffee, heard her singing. Grant was struck with a powerful wave of *déjà vu*. He could explain it, he told himself he could explain it because it had been just like this the first morning after he'd met her. But it wasn't that—that was much, much too logical for the strength of the feeling that swamped him. It was more than an already seen—it was a sensation of rightness, of always, of pleasure so simple it stung. If he walked into that kitchen a hundred times, year after year, it would never seem balanced, never seem whole, unless she was waiting for him.

Grant paused in the doorway to watch her. The coffee was hot and ready as she stretched up for the mugs that he could reach easily. The sun shot light into her hair, teasing out those deep red hints until they shimmered, flame on velvet. She turned, catching her breath in surprise when she saw him, then smiling.

"I didn't hear you come down." She swung her hair behind her shoulder as she began to pour coffee. "It's gorgeous out. The rain's got everything gleaming and the ocean's more blue than green. You wouldn't know there'd ever been a storm." Taking a mug in each hand, she turned back to him. Though she'd intended to cross to him, the look in his eyes stopped her. Puzzlement quickly became tension. Was he angry? she wondered. Why? Perhaps he was already regretting what had happened. Why had she been so foolish as to think what had been between them had been as special, as unique for him as it had been for her?

Her fingers tightened on the handles. She wouldn't let him apologize, make excuses. She wouldn't cause a scene. The pain was real, physically real, but she told herself to ignore it. Later, when she was alone, she would deal with it. But now she would face him without tears, without pleas.

"Is something wrong?" Was that her voice, so calm, so controlled?

"Yeah, something's wrong."

Her fingers held the mugs so tightly she wondered that the handles didn't snap off. Still, it kept her hands from shaking. "Maybe we should sit down."

"I don't want to sit down." His voice was sharp as a slap but she didn't flinch. She watched as he paced to the sink and leaned against it, muttering and swearing. Another time the Grantlike gesture would have amused her, but now he only stood and waited. If he was going to hurt her, let him do it quickly, at once, before she fell apart. He whirled, almost violently, and stared at her accusingly. "Damn it, Gennie, I've had my head lopped off."

It was her turn to stare. Her fingers went numb against the stoneware. Her pulse seemed to stop long enough to make her head swim before it began to race. The color drained from her face until it was like porcelain against the glowing green of her eyes. On another oath, Grant dragged a hand through his hair.

"You're spilling the coffee," he muttered, then stuck his hands in his pockets.

"Oh." Gennie looked down foolishly at the tiny twin puddles that were forming on the floor, then set down the mugs. "I'll—I'll wipe it up."

"Leave it." Grant grabbed her arm before she could reach for a towel. "Listen, I feel like someone's just given me a solid right straight to the gut—the kind that doubles you over and makes your head ring at the same time. I feel that way too often when I look at you." When she said nothing, he took her other arm and shook. "In the first place I never asked to have you walk into my life and mess up my head. The last thing I wanted was for you to get in my way, but you did. So now I'm in love with you, and I can tell you, I'm not crazy about the idea."

Gennie found her voice, though she wasn't quite certain what to do with it. "Well," she managed after a moment, "that certainly puts me in my place."

"Oh, she wants to make jokes." Disgusted, Grant released her to storm over to the coffee. Lifting a mug, he drained half the contents, perversely pleased that it scalded his throat. "Well, laugh this off," he suggested as he slammed the mug down again and glared. "You're not going anywhere until I figure out what the hell I'm going to do about you."

Struggling against conflicting emotions of amusement, annoyance, and simple wonder, she put her hands on her hips. The movement shifted the too-big robe so that it threatened to slip off of one shoulder. "Oh, really? So you're going to figure out what to do about me, like I was an inconvenient head cold."

"Damned inconvenient," he muttered.

"You may not have noticed, but I'm a grown woman with a mind of my own, accustomed to making my own decisions. You're not going to *do* anything about me," she told him as her temper began to overtake everything else. She jabbed a finger at him, and the gap in the robe widened. "If you're in love with me, that's your problem. I have one of my own because I'm in love with you."

"Terrific!" he shouted at her. "That's just terrific. We'd both have been better off if you'd waited out that storm in a ditch instead of coming here."

"You're not telling me anything I don't already know," Gennie retorted, then spun around to leave the room.

"Just a minute." Grant had her arm again and backed her into the wall. "You're not going anywhere until this is settled."

"It's settled!" Tossing her hair out of her face, she glared at him. "We're in love with each other and I wish you'd go jump off that cliff. If you had any finesse—"

"I don't."

"Any sensitivity," she continued, "you wouldn't announce that you were in love with someone in the same tone you'd use to frighten small children."

"I'm not in love with someone!" he shouted at her, infuriated because she was right and he couldn't do a thing about it. "I'm in love with you, and damn it, I don't like it."

"You've made that abundantly clear." She straightened her shoulders and lifted her chin.

"Don't pull that regal routine on me," Grant began. Her eyes sharpened to dagger points. Her skin flushed majestically. Abruptly he began to laugh. When she tossed her head back in fury, he simply collapsed against her. "Oh, God, Gennie, I can't take it when you look at me as though you were about to have me tossed in the dungeon."

"Get off of me, you ass!" Incensed, insulted, she shoved against him, but he only held her tighter. Only quick reflexes saved him from a well-aimed knee at a strategic point.

"Hold on." Still chuckling, he pressed his mouth to hers. Then as abruptly as his laughter had begun, it stilled. With the gentleness he so rarely showed, his hands came up to frame her face, and she was lost. "Gennie." With his lips still on hers he murmured her name so that the sound of it shivered through her. "I love you." He combed his fingers through her hair, drawing her head back so that their eyes met. "I don't like it, I may never get used to it, but I love you." With a sigh, he brought her close again. "You make my head swim."

With her cheek against his chest, Gennie closed her eyes. "You can take time to get used to it," she murmured. "Just promise you won't ever be sorry it happened."

"Not sorry," he agreed on a long breath. "A little crazed, but not sorry." As he ran a hand down her hair, Grant felt a fresh need for her, softer, calmer than before but no less vibrant. He nuzzled into her neck because he seemed to belong there. "Are you really in love with me, or did you say that because I made you mad?"

"Both. I decided this morning I'd have to bend to your ego and let you tell me first."

"Is that so?" With his brows drawn together, he tilted her head back again. "My ego."

"It tends to get in the way because it's rather oversized." She smiled, sweetly. In retaliation, he crushed his mouth to hers.

"You know," he managed after a moment. "I've lost my appetite for breakfast."

Smiling again, she tilted her face back to his. "Have you really?"

"Mmmm. And I don't like to mention it..." He took his fingertips to the lapel of the robe, toying with it before he slid them down to the belt. "But I didn't say you could use my robe."

"Oh, that was rude of me." The smile became saucy. "Would you like it back now?"

"No hurry." He slipped his hand into hers and started toward the steps. "You can wait until we get upstairs."

From his bedroom window, Grant watched her drive away. It was early afternoon now, and the sun was brilliant. He needed some distance from her—perhaps she needed some from him as well. That's what he told himself even while he wondered how long he could stay away.

There was work waiting for him in the studio above his head, a routine he knew was directly connected to the quality and quantity of his output. He needed that one strict discipline in his life, the hours out of the day and night that were guided by his creativity and his drive. Yet how could he work when his mind was so full of her, when his body was still warm from hers?

Love. He'd managed to avoid it for so many years, then he had thoughtlessly opened the door. It had barged in on him, Grant reflected, uninvited, unwelcomed. Now he was vulnerable, dependent—all the things he'd once promised himself he'd never be again. If he could change it, he was sure he would. He had lived by his own rules, his own judgment, his own needs for so long he wasn't certain he was willing or able to make the compromises love entailed.

He would end up hurting her, Grant thought grimly, and the pain would ricochet back on him. That was the inevitable fate of all lovers. What did they want from each other? Shaking his head, Grant turned from the window. For now, time and affection were enough, but that would change. What would happen when the demands crept in, the strings? Would he bolt? He had no business falling in love with someone like Gennie, whose life-style was light-years away from the one he had chosen, whose very innocence made her that much more susceptible to hurt.

She'd never be content to live with him there on his isolated finger of land, and he'd never ask her to. He couldn't give up his peace for the parties, the cameras, the social whirl. If he'd been more like Shelby...

Grant thought of his sister and her love for crowds, people, noise. Each of them had compensated in their own way for the trauma of losing their father in such a hideous, public fashion. But after fifteen years, the scars were still there. Perhaps Shelby had healed more cleanly, or perhaps her love for Alan MacGregor was strong enough to overcome that nagging fear. The fear of exposure, of losing, of depending.

He remembered Shelby's visit to him before she made her decision to marry Alan. She'd been miserable, afraid. He'd been rough on her because he'd wanted to hold her, to let her weep out the memories that haunted them both. He'd spoken the truth because the truth was what she'd needed to hear, but Grant wasn't certain he could live by it.

"Are you going to shut yourself off from life because of something that happened fifteen years ago?"

He'd asked her that, scathingly, when she'd sat in his kitchen with her eyes brimming over. And he remembered her angry, intuitive, *"Haven't you?"*

In his own way he had, though his work and the love of it kept him permanently connected with the world. He drew for people, for their pleasure and entertainment, because in a fashion perhaps only he himself understood, he liked them—their flaws and strengths, their foolishness and sanity. He simply wouldn't be crowded by them. And he'd refused, successfully until Gennie, to be too deeply involved with anyone on a one to one level. It was so simple to deal with humanity on a general scope. The pitfalls occurred when you narrowed it down.

Pitfalls, he thought with a snort. He'd fallen into a big one. He was already impatient to have her back with him, to hear her voice, to see her smile at him.

She'd be setting up now for the watercolor she'd told him she was going to begin. Maybe she'd still be wearing the shirt Grant had lent her. Her own had been torn beyond repair. Without effort, he could picture her setting up her easel near the inlet. Her hair would be brushed away from her face to fall behind her. His shirt would be hanging past her hips...

And while she was getting her work done, he was standing around mooning like a teenager. On a sound of frustration, Grant strode into the hall just as the phone began to ring. He started to ignore it, something he did easily, then changed his mind and loped down the stairs. He kept only one phone, in the kitchen, because he refused to be disturbed by anything while he was in his studio or in his bed. Grant snatched the receiver from the wall and leaned against the doorway.

"Yeah?"

"Grant Campbell?"

Though he'd only met the man once, Grant had no trouble identifying the voice. It was distinctive, even without the slight slur it cast on the *Campbell*. "Hello, Daniel."

"You're a hard man to reach. Been out of town?"

"No." Grant grinned. "I don't always answer the phone."

The snort Daniel gave caused Grant's grin to widen. He could imagine the big MacGregor sitting in his private tower room, smoking one of his forbidden cigars behind his massive desk. Grant had caricatured him just that way, then had slipped the sketch to Shelby during her wedding reception. Absently he reached for a bag of corn chips on the counter and ripped them open.

"How are you?"

"Fine. More than fine." Daniel's booming voice took on hints of pride and arrogance. "I'm a grandfather—two weeks ago."

"Congratulations."

"A boy," Daniel informed him, taking a satisfied puff on his thick, Cuban cigar. "Seven pounds, four ounces, strong as a bull. Robert MacGregor Blade. They'll be calling him Mac. Good stock." He took a deep breath that strained the buttons on his shirt. "The boy has my ears."

Grant listened to the rundown on the newest MacGregor with a mixture of amusement and affection. His sister had married into a family that he personally found irresistible. He knew pieces of them would be popping up in his strip for years to come. "How's Rena?"

"Came through like a champ." Daniel bit down on his cigar. "Of course, I knew she would. Her mother was worried. Females."

He didn't mention it was he who had insisted on chartering a plane the minute he'd learned Serena had gone into labor. Or that he had paced the waiting room like a madman while his wife, Anna, had calmly finished the embroidery on a baby blanket.

"Justin stayed with her the whole time." There was just a touch of resentment in the words—enough to tell Grant the hospital staff had barred the Mac-Gregor's way into the delivery room. And probably hadn't had an easy time of it.

"Has Shelby seen her nephew yet?"

"Off on their honeymoon during the birthing," Daniel told him with a wheezy sigh. It was difficult for him to understand why his son and daughter-in-law hadn't canceled their plans to be on hand for such a momentous occasion. "But then, she and Alan are making up for it this weekend. That's why I called. We want you to come down, boy. The whole family's coming, the new babe, too. Anna's fretting to have all the children around again. You know how women are."

He knew how Daniel was, and grinned again. "Mothers need to fuss, I imagine."

"Aye, that's it. And with a new generation started, she'll be worse than ever." Daniel cast a wary eye at his closed door. You never knew when someone might be listening. "Now, then, you'll come, Friday night."

Grant thought of his schedule and did some quick mental figuring. He had an urge to see his sister again, and the MacGregors. More, he felt the need to take Gennie to the people whom, without knowing why, he considered family. "I could come down for a couple of days, Daniel, but I'd like to bring someone."

"Someone?" Daniel's senses sharpened. He leaned forward with the cigar smoldering in his hand. "Who might this someone be?"

Recognizing the tone, Grant crunched on a corn chip. "An artist I know who's doing some painting in

New England, in Windy Point at the moment. I think she'd be interested in your house.''

She, Daniel thought with an irrepressible grin. Just because he'd managed to comfortably establish his children didn't mean he had to give up the satisfying hobby of matchmaking. Young people needed to be guided in such matters—or shoved along. And Grant—though he was a Campbell—was by way of being family...

"An artist...aye, that's interesting. Always room for one more, son. Bring her along. An artist,'' he repeated, tapping out his cigar. "Young and pretty, too, I'm sure.''

"She's nearly seventy,'' Grant countered easily, crossing his ankles as he leaned against the wall. "A little dumpy, has a face like a frog. Her paintings are timeless, tremendous emotional content and physicality. I'm crazy about her.'' He paused, imagining Daniel's wide face turning a deep puce. "Genuine emotion transcends age and physical beauty, don't you agree?''

Daniel choked, then found his voice. The boy needed help, a great deal of help. "You come early Friday, son. We'll need some time to talk.'' He stared hard at the bookshelf across the room. "Seventy, you say?''

"Close. But then true sensuality is ageless. Why just last night she and I—''

"No, don't tell me,'' Daniel interrupted hastily. "We'll have a long talk when you get here. A long talk,'' he added after a deep breath. "Has Shelby met— No, never mind,'' he decided. "Friday,'' Daniel said in a firmer tone. "We'll see about all this on Friday.''

"We'll be there." Grant hung up, then leaning against the doorjamb, laughed until he hurt. That should keep the old boy on his toes until Friday, Grant thought. Still grinning, he headed for the stairs. He'd work until dark—until Gennie.

Chapter Nine

Gennie had never known herself to be talked into anything so quickly. Before she knew what was happening, she was agreeing to pack her painting gear and a suitcase and fly off to spend a weekend with people she didn't know.

Part of the reason, she realized when she had a moment to sort it out, was that Grant was enthusiastic about the MacGregors. She learned enough about him in little more than a week to know that he rarely felt genuine affection for anyone—enough affection at any rate to give up his precious privacy and his time. She had agreed primarily because she simply wanted to be where he was, next because she was caught up in his pleasure. And finally because she wanted to see him under a different set of circumstances, interacting with people, away from his isolated spot on the globe.

She would meet his sister. The fact that he had one had come as a surprise. Though she admitted it was foolish, Gennie had had a picture of Grant simply popping into the world as an adult, by himself, already prepared to fight for the right to his place and his privacy.

Now she began to wonder about his childhood—what had formed him? What had made him into the Grant Campbell she knew? Had he been rich or poor, outgoing or introverted? Had he been happy, loved, ignored? He rarely talked about his family, his past...for that matter, of his present.

Oddly, because the answers were so important, she couldn't ask the questions. Gennie found she needed that step to come from him, as proof of the love he said he felt. No, perhaps proof was the wrong word, she mused. She believed he loved her, in his way, but she wanted the seal. To her, there was no separating trust from love, because one without the other was just an empty word. She didn't believe in secrets.

From childhood until her sister's death, Gennie had had that one special person to share everything with—all her doubts, insecurities, wishes, dreams. Losing Angela had been like losing part of herself, a part she was only beginning to feel again. It was the most natural thing in the world for her to give that trust and affection to Grant. Where she loved, she loved without boundaries.

Beneath the joy she felt was a quiet ache that came from knowing he had yet to open to her. Until he did, Gennie felt their future extended no further than the moment. She forced herself to accept that, because the thought of the moment without him was unbearable.

Grant glanced over as he turned onto the narrow cliff road that led to the MacGregor estate. He glimpsed Gennie's profile, the quiet expression, the eyes dreamy and not quite happy. ''What're you thinking?''

She turned her head, and with her smile the wisp of sadness vanished. ''That I love you.''

It was so simple. It made his knees weak. Needing to touch her, Grant pulled onto the shoulder of the road and stopped. She was still smiling when he cupped her face in his hands, and her lashes lowered in anticipation of the kiss.

Softly, with a reverence he never expected to feel, he brushed his lips over her cheeks, first one, then the other. Her breath caught in her throat to lodge with her heart. His rare spurts of gentleness never failed to undo her. Anything, everything he might have asked of her at that moment, she would have given without hesitation. The whisper of his lashes against her skin bound her to him more firmly than any chain.

Her name was only a sigh as he trailed kisses over her closed lids. With her tremble, his thoughts began to swirl. What was this magic she cast over him? It glittered one instant, then pulsed the next. Was it only his imagination, or had she always been there, waiting to spring into his life and make him a slave? Was it her softness or her strength that made him want to kill or to die for her? Did it matter?

He knew it should. When a man got pulled in too deeply—by a woman, an ideal, a goal—he became vulnerable. Then the instinct for survival would take second place. Grant had always understood this was what had happened to his father.

But now all he could grasp was that she was so soft, so giving. His.

Lightly, Grant touched his lips to hers. Gennie tilted back her head and opened to him. His fingers tightened on her, his breath quickened, rushing into her mouth just before his tongue. The transition from gentle to desperate was too swift to be measured. Her fingers tangled in his hair to drag him closer while he ravished a mouth more demanding than willing. Caught in the haze, Gennie thought her passion rose higher and faster each time he touched her until one day she would simply explode from a mere look.

"I want you." She felt the words wrench from her. As they slipped from her mouth into his, he crushed her against him in a grip that left all gentleness behind. His lips savaged, warred, absorbed, until they were both speechless. With an inarticulate murmur, Grant buried his face in her hair and fought to find reason.

"Good God, in another minute I'll forget it's still daylight and this is a public road."

Gennie ran her fingers down the nape of his neck. "I already have."

Grant forced the breath in and out of his lungs three times, then lifted his head. "Be careful," he warned quietly. "I have a more difficult time remembering to be civilized than doing what comes naturally. At this moment I'd feel very natural dragging you into the back seat, tearing off your clothes, and loving you until you were senseless."

A thrill rushed up and down her spine, daring her, urging her. She leaned closer until her lips were nearly against his. "One should never go against one's nature."

"Gennie..." His control was so thinly balanced, he could already feel the way her body would heat and soften beneath his. Her scent contradicted the lowering sun and whispered of midnight. When she slid her hands up his chest, he could hear his own heartbeat vibrate against her palm. Her eyes were clouded, yet somehow they held more power. Grant couldn't look away from them. He saw himself a prisoner, exulting in the weight of the chains.

Just as the scales tipped away from reason, the sound of an approaching engine had him swearing and turning his head. Gennie looked over her shoulder as a Mercedes pulled to a halt beside them. The driver was in shadows, so that she had only the impression of dark, masculine looks while the passenger rolled down her window.

A cap of wild red hair surrounding an angular face poked out the opening. The woman leaned her arms on the base of the window and grinned appealingly. "You people lost?"

Grant sent her a narrow-eyed glare, then astonished Gennie by reaching out and twisting her nose between his first two fingers. "Scram."

"Some people just aren't worth helping," the woman stated before she gave a haughty toss of her head and disappeared back inside. The Mercedes purred discreetly, then disappeared around the first curve.

"Grant!" Torn between amusement and disbelief, Gennie stared at him. "Even for you that was unbelievably rude."

"Can't stand busybodies," he said easily as he started the car again.

She let out a gusty sigh as she flopped back against the cushions. "You certainly made that clear enough. I'm beginning to think it was a miracle you didn't just slam the door in my face that first night."

"It was a weak moment."

She slanted a look at him, then gave up. "How close are we? You might want to run off the cast of characters for me so I'll have an idea who…" She trailed off. "Oh, God."

It was incredible, impossible. Wonderful. Stark gray in the last lights of the sun, it was the fairy castle every little girl imagined herself trapped in. It would take a valiant knight to free her from the high stone walls of the tower. That it was here, in this century of rockets and rushing was a miracle in itself.

The structure jutted and spread, and quite simply dominated the cliff on which it stood. No ivy clung to its walls. What ivy would dare encroach? But there were flowers—wild roses, blooms in brambles, haunting colors that stubbornly shouted of summer while the nearby trees were edged with the first breath of fall.

Gennie didn't simply want to paint it. She had to paint it in essentially the same way she had to breathe.

"I thought so," Grant commented.

Dazed, Gennie continued to stare. "What?"

"You might as well have a brush in your hand already."

"I only wish I did."

"If you paint this with half the insight and the power you used in your study of the cliffs and lighthouse, you'll have a magnificent piece of work."

Gennie turned to him then, confused. "But I—you didn't seem to think too much of the painting."

He snorted as he negotiated the last curve. "Don't be an idiot."

It never occurred to him that she would need reassurance. Grant knew his own skills, and accepted with a shrug the fact that he was considered one of the top in his field. What others thought mattered little, because he knew his own capabilities. He assumed Gennie would feel precisely the same about herself.

If he had known the agony she went through before each of her showings, he would have been flabbergasted. If he had known just how much he had hurt her by his casual comment the day she had finished the painting, he would have been speechless.

Gennie frowned at him, concentrating. "You did like it, then?"

"Like what?"

"The painting," she snapped impatiently. "The painting I did in your front yard."

With their minds working at cross purposes, Grant didn't hear the insecurity in the demand. "Just because I don't paint," he began curtly, "doesn't mean I have to be slugged over the head with genius to recognize it."

They lapsed into silence, neither one certain of the other's mood, or their own.

If he liked the painting, Gennie fumed, why didn't he just say so instead of making her drag it out of him?

Grant wondered if she thought *serious* art was the only worthwhile medium. What the hell would she have to say if he told her he made his living by depicting people as he saw them through cartoons? Funny papers. Would she laugh or throw a fit if she caught a glimpse of his Veronica in the New York *Daily* in a couple of weeks?

They pulled up in front of the house with a jerk of brakes that brought them both back to the moment. "Wait until we get inside," he began, picking up the threads of their earlier conversation. "I only believed half of what I saw myself."

"Apparently everything I've ever read or heard about Daniel MacGregor's true." Gennie stepped out of the car with her eyes trained on the house again. "Forceful, eccentric, a man who makes his own deals his own way. But I'm vague on personal details. His wife's a doctor?"

"Surgeon. There're three children, and as you'll be hearing innumerable times over the weekend, one grandson. My sister married the eldest son, Alan."

"Alan MacGregor... He's—"

"Senator MacGregor, and in a few years..." With a shrug, he trailed off.

"Ah, yes, you'd have a direct line into the White House if the murmurs about Alan MacGregor's aspirations become fact." She grinned at the man in khakis leaning against the hood of the rented car while the wind played games with his hair. "How would you feel about that?"

Grant gave her an odd smile, thinking of Macintosh. "Things are presently unsettled," he murmured. "But I've always had a rather—wry affection for politics in general." Grabbing her hand, he began to walk toward the rough stone steps. "Then there's Caine, son number two, a lawyer who recently married another lawyer who as it happens, is the sister of Daniel's youngest offspring's husband."

"I'm not sure I'm keeping up." Gennie studied the brass-crowned lion's head that served as a door knocker.

"You have to be a quick study." Grant lifted the knocker and let it fall resoundingly. "Rena married a gambler. She and her husband own a number of casinos and live in Atlantic City."

Gennie gave him a thoughtful glance. "For someone who keeps to himself so much, you're well informed."

"Yeah." He grinned at her as the door opened.

The redhead that Gennie recognized from the Mercedes leaned against the thick panel and looked Grant up and down. "Still lost?"

This time Grant tugged her against him and gave her a hard kiss. "Apparently you've survived a month of matrimony, but you're still skinny."

"And compliments still roll trippingly off your tongue," she retorted, drawing back. After a moment she laughed and hugged him fiercely. "Damn, I hate to say it out loud, but it's good to see you." Grinning over Grant's shoulder, she pinned Ginnie with a curious, not unfriendly glance. "Hi, I'm Shelby."

Grant's sister, Gennie realized, thrown off by the total lack of any familial resemblance. She had the impression of hordes of energy inside a long lean body, unruly fiery curls, and smoky eyes. While Grant had a rugged, unkempt attractiveness, his sister was a combination of porcelain and flame.

"I'm Gennie." She responded instinctively to the smile Shelby shot her before she untangled herself from her brother. "I'm glad to meet you."

"Pushing seventy, hmmm?" Shelby said cryptically to Grant before she clasped Gennie's hand. "We'll have to get to know each other so you can tell me how you tolerate this jerk's company for more than five minutes at a time. Alan's in the throne room with the MacGregor," she continued before Grant could retort. "Has Grant given you a rundown on the inmates?"

"An abbreviated version," Gennie replied, instantly charmed.

"Typical." She hooked her arm through Gennie's. "Well, sometimes it's best to jump in feet first. The most important thing to remember is not to let Daniel intimidate you. What extraction are you?"

"French mostly. Why?"

"It'll come up."

"How was the honeymoon?" Grant demanded, wanting to veer away from the subject that would, indeed, come up.

Shelby beamed at him. "I'll let you know when it's over. How's your cliff?"

"Still standing." He glanced to his left as Justin started down the main stairs. Justin's expression of mild curiosity changed to surprise—something rarely seen on his face—then pleasure.

"Gennie!" He took the rest of the stairs in quick, long strides then whirled her into his arms.

"Justin." Laughing, she hooked her arms around his neck while Grant's eyes narrowed to slits.

"What're you doing here?" they asked together.

Chuckling, he took both of her hands, drawing back for a long, thorough study. "You're beautiful," he told her. "Always."

Grant watched her flush with pleasure and experienced the first genuine jealousy of his life. He found it a very unpleasant sensation. "It seems," he said in a dangerously mild voice that had Shelby's brows lifting, "you two have met."

"Yes, of course," Gennie began before realization dawned. "The gambler!" she exclaimed. "Oh, I never put it together. Rena—Serena. Hearing you were getting married was a shock in itself, I hated to miss the wedding...and a father!" She threw her arms around him again, laughing. "Good God, I'm surrounded by cousins."

"Cousins?" Grant echoed.

"On my French side," Justin said wryly. "A distant connection, carefully overlooked by all but a—" he tilted Gennie's face to his "—select few."

"Aunt Adelaide's a stuffy old bore," Gennie said precisely.

"Are you following this?" Shelby asked Grant.

"Barely," he muttered.

With another laugh, Gennie held out her hand to him. "To keep it simple, Justin and I are cousins, third, I think. We happened to meet about five years ago at one of my shows in New York."

"I wasn't—ah—close to that particular end of my family," Justin continued. "Some chance comment led to another until we ferreted out the connection."

When Justin smiled down at Gennie, Grant saw it. The eyes, the green eyes. Man, woman, they were almost identical to the shade. For some obscure reason that, more than the explanations, had him relaxing the muscles that had gone taut the moment Justin had scooped her up. The black sheep, he realized, who'd outdone them all.

"Fascinating," Shelby decided. "All those clichés about small worlds are amazingly apt. Gennie's here with Grant."

"Oh?" Justin glanced over, meeting Grant's dark, appraising eyes. As a gambler he habitually sized up the people he met and stored them into compartments. At Shelby's wedding the month before, Justin had found him a man with wit and secrets who refused to be stored anywhere. They'd gotten along easily, perhaps because the need for privacy was inherent in both of them. Now, remembering Daniel's blustering description of Grant's weekend companion, Justin controlled a grin. "Daniel mentioned you were bringing—an artist."

Grant recognized, as few would have, the gleam of humor in Justin's eyes. "I'm sure he did," he returned in the same conversational tone. "I haven't congratulated you yet on ensuring the continuity of the line."

"And saving the rest of us from the pressure to do so immediately," Shelby finished.

"Don't count on it," a smooth voice warned.

Gennie looked up to see a blond woman descending the steps, carrying a bundle in a blue blanket.

"Hello, Grant. It's nice to see you again." Serena cradled her son in one arm as she leaned over to kiss Grant's cheek. "It was sweet of you to answer the royal summons."

"My pleasure." Unable to resist, he nudged the blanket aside with a finger.

So little. Babies had always held a fascination for him—their perfection in miniature. This one was smooth-cheeked and wide awake, staring back at him with dark blue eyes he thought already hinted of the violet of his mother's. Perhaps Mac had Daniel's ears and Serena's eyes, but the rest of him was pure Blade. He had the bones of a warrior, Grant thought, and the striking black hair of his Comanche blood.

Looking beyond her son, Serena studied the woman who was watching Grant with a quiet thoughtfulness. It surprised her to see her husband's eyes in a feminine face. Waiting until those eyes shifted to hers, she smiled. "I'm Rena."

"Gennie's a friend of Grant's," Justin announced, easily slipping an arm around his wife's shoulders. "She also happens to be my cousin." Before Serena could react to the first surprise, he hit her with the second. "Genviève Grandeau."

"Oh, those marvelous paintings!" she exclaimed while Shelby's eyes widened.

"Damn it, Grant." After giving him a disgusted look, Shelby turned to Gennie. "Our mother had two of your landscapes. I badgered her into giving me one as a wedding present. *Evening*," she elaborated. "I want to build a house around it."

Pleased, Gennie smiled at her. "Then maybe you'll help me convince Mr. MacGregor that I should paint his house."

"Just watch how you have to twist his arm," Serena said dryly.

"What is this, a summit meeting?" Alan demanded as he strode down the hall. "It's one thing to be the advance man," he continued as he cupped a hand around the back of his wife's neck, "and another to be the sacrificial lamb. Dad's doing a lot of moaning and groaning about this family scattering off in all directions."

"With Caine getting the worst of it," Serena put in.

"Yeah." Alan grinned once, appealingly. "Too bad he's late." His gaze shifted to Gennie then—dark, intense eyes, a slow, serious smile. "We've met..." He hesitated briefly as he flipped through his mental file of names and faces. "Genviève Grandeau."

A little surprised, Gennie smiled back at him. "A very quick meeting at a very crowded charity function about two years ago, senator."

"Alan," he corrected. "So you're Grant's artist." He sent Grant a look that had lights of humor softening his eyes. "I must say you outshine even Grant's description of you. Shall we all go in and join the MacGregor before he starts to bellow?"

"Here." Justin took the baby from Serena in an expert move. "Mac'll soften him up."

"What description?" Gennie murmured to Grant as they started down the wide hall.

She saw the grin tug at his mouth before he slipped an arm around her shoulders. "Later."

Gennie immediately saw why Shelby had referred to it as the throne room. The expansive floor space was covered with a scarlet rug. All the woodwork was lushly carved while magnificent paintings hung in ornate frames. There was the faint smell of candlewax, though no candles were lit. Lamps glowed to aid the soft light of dusk that trailed in the many mullioned windows.

She saw at a glance that the furniture was ancient and wonderful, all large-scaled and perfect in the enormous room. Logs were laid and ready in the huge fireplace in anticipation of the chill that could come during the evenings when summer warred with autumn.

But the room, superb in its unique fashion, was nothing compared to the man holding court from his high-backed Gothic chair. Massive, with red hair thick and flaming, he watched the procession file into the room with narrowed, sharp blue eyes in a wide, lined face.

To Gennie, he looked like a general or a king—both, perhaps, in the way of centuries past where the monarch led his people into battle. One huge hand tapped the wooden arm of his chair while the other held a glass half-filled with liquid. He looked fierce enough to order executions arbitrarily. Her fingers itched for a pad and a pencil.

"Well," he said in a deep, rumbling voice that made the syllable an accusation.

Shelby was the first to go to him, bravely, Gennie thought, to give him a smacking kiss on the mouth. "Hi, Grandpa."

He reddened at that and struggled with the pleasure the title gave him. "So you decided to give me a moment of your time."

"I felt duty bound to pay my respects to the newest MacGregor first."

As if on cue, Justin strode over to arrange Mac in the crook of Daniel's arm. Gennie watched the fierce giant turn into a marshmallow. "There's a laddie," he crooned, holding out his glass to Shelby, then chucking the baby under the chin. When the baby grabbed his thick finger, he preened like a rooster. "Strong as an ox." He grinned foolishly at the room in general, then zeroed in on Grant. "Well, Campbell, so you've come. You see here," he began, jiggling the baby, "why the MacGregors could never be conquered. Strong stock."

"Good blood," Serena murmured, taking the baby from the proud grandfather.

"Get a drink for the Campbell," he ordered. "Now, where's this artist?" His eyes darted around the room, landed on Gennie and clung. She thought she saw surprise, quickly veiled, then amusement as quickly suppressed, tug at the corners of his mouth.

"Daniel MacGregor," Grant said with wry formality, "Geneviève Grandeau."

A flicker of recognition ran across Daniel's face before he rose to his rather amazing height and held out his hand. "Welcome."

Gennie's hand was clasped, then enveloped. She had simultaneous impressions of strength, compassion, and stubbornness.

"You have a magnificent home, Mr. MacGregor," she said, studying him candidly. "It suits you."

He gave a great bellow of a laugh that might have shook the windows. "Aye. And three of your paintings hang in the west wing." His eyes slid briefly to Grant's before they came back to hers. "You carry your age well, lass."

She gave him a puzzled look as Grant choked over his Scotch. "Thank you."

"Get the artist a drink," he ordered, then gestured for her to sit in the chair next to his. "Now, tell me why you're wasting your time with a Campbell."

"Gennie happens to be a cousin of mine," Justin said mildly as he sat on the sofa beside his son. "On the aristocratic French side."

"A cousin." Daniel's eyes sharpened, then an expression that could only be described as cunning pleasure spread over his face. "Aye, we like to keep things in the family. Grandeau—a good strong name. You've the look of a queen, with a bit of sorceress thrown in."

"That was meant as a compliment," Serena told her as she handed Gennie a vermouth in crystal.

"So I've been told." Gennie sent Grant an easy look over the rim of her glass. "One of my ancestors had an—encounter with a gypsy resulting in twins."

"Gennie has a pirate in her family tree as well," Justin put in.

Daniel nodded in approval. "Strong blood. The Campbells need all the help they can get."

"Watch it, MacGregor," Shelby warned as Grant gave him a brief, fulminating look.

There were undercurrents here to confuse a newcomer, but not so subtle Gennie didn't catch the drift. He's trying to arrange a betrothal, she thought, and struggled with a chuckle. Seeing Grant's dark, annoyed look only made it more difficult to maintain her composure. The game was irresistible. "The Grandeaus can trace their ancestry back to a favored courtesan of Philip IV le Bel." She caught Shelby's look of amused respect. In the time it took for eyes to meet, a bond was formed.

Though he was enjoying the signals being flashed around the room, Alan remembered all too well being in the position Grant was currently...enjoying. "I wonder what's keeping Caine," he said casually, aware how the comment would shift his father's focus.

"Hah!" Daniel downed half his drink in one swallow. "The boy's too bound up in his law to give his mother a moment's thought."

At Gennie's lifted brows, Serena curled her legs under her. "My mother's still at the hospital," she explained, a smile lurking around her mouth. "I'm sure she'll be devastated if she arrives before Caine does."

"She worries about her children," Daniel put in with a sniff. "I try to tell her that they have lives of their own to lead, but a mother's a mother."

Serena rolled her eyes and said something inarticulate into her glass. It was enough, however, to make Daniel's face flush. Before he could retort, the sound of the knocker thudding against wood vibrated against the walls.

"I'll get it," Alan said, feeling that would give him a moment to warn Caine of their father's barometer.

Because he felt a certain kinship with Caine at that moment, Grant turned to Daniel in an attempt to shift his mood. "Gennie was fascinated by the house," he began. "She's hoping to persuade you into letting her paint it."

Daniel's reaction was immediate. Not unlike his reaction to his grandson, he preened. "Well, now, we should be able to arrange something that suits us both."

A Grandeau of the MacGregor fortress. He knew the financial value of such a painting, not to mention the value to his pride. The legacy for his grandchildren.

"We'll talk," he said with a decisive nod just as the latest MacGregors came into the room. Daniel cast a look in their direction. "Hah!"

Gennie saw a tall, lean man with the air of an intelligent wolf stroll in. Were all the MacGregors such superb examples of the human species? she wondered. There was power there, the same as she had sensed in Alan and Serena. Because it wasn't wholly the same as Daniel's, Gennie speculated on their mother. Just what sort of woman was she?

Then her attention was caught by the woman who entered with Caine. Justin's sister. Gennie glanced at her cousin to see him eyeing his sister with a slight frown. And she understood why. The tension Caine and Diana had brought into the room was palpable.

"We got held up in Boston," Caine said easily, shrugging off his father's scowl before he walked over to look at his nephew. The rather hard lines of his face softened when he glanced up at his sister. "Good job, Rena."

"You might call when you're going to be late," Daniel stated. "So your mother wouldn't worry."

Caine took in the room with a sweeping glance, noticing his mother's absence, then lifted an ironic brow. "Of course."

"It's my fault," Diana said in a low voice. "An appointment ran over."

"You remember Grant," Serena began, hoping to smooth over what looked like very rough edges.

"Yes, of course." Diana managed a smile that didn't reach her large, dark eyes.

"And Grant's guest," Serena continued with the wish that she could have a few moments alone with Diana. "Who turns out to be a cousin of yours, Genviève Grandeau."

Diana stiffened instantly, her face cool and expressionless when she turned to Gennie.

"Cousin?" Caine said curiously as he moved to stand beside his wife.

"Yes." Gennie spoke up, wanting to ease something she didn't understand. "We met once," she went on, offering a smile, "when we were children, at a birthday party, I think. My family was in Boston, visiting."

"I remember," Diana murmured.

Though she tried, Gennie could remember nothing she had done at the silly little party to warrant the cool, remote look Diana gave her. Her reaction was instinctive. Her chin angled slightly, her brows arched. With the regal look settling over her, she sipped her vermouth. "As Shelby pointed out, it's a small world."

Caine recognized Diana's expression, and though it exasperated him, he laid a reassuring hand on her shoulder. "Welcome, cousin," he said to Gennie, giving her an unexpectedly charming smile. He turned to Grant then, and the smile tilted mischievously. "I'd really like to talk to you—about frogs."

Grant responded with a lightning fast grin. "Anytime."

Before Gennie could even begin to sort this out, or the laughter that followed it, a small, dark woman came into the room. Here was the other end of the power. Gennie sensed it immediately as the woman became the center of attention. There was a strength about her, and the serious, attractive looks that she had passed on to her eldest son. She carried a strange dignity, though her hair was slightly mussed and her suit just a bit wrinkled.

"I'm so glad you could come," she said to Gennie when they were introduced. Her hands were small and capable, and Gennie discovered, chilled. "I'm sorry I wasn't here when you arrived. I was—detained at the hospital."

She's lost a patient. Without knowing how she understood it, Gennie was certain. Instinctively, she covered their joined hands with her free one. "You have a wonderful family, Mrs. MacGregor. A beautiful grandson."

Anna let out a tiny sigh that was hardly audible. "Thank you." She moved to brush a kiss over her husband's cheek."Let's go in to dinner," she said when he patted her hair. "You all must be starving by now."

The cast of characters was complete, Gennie mused as she rose to take Grant's hand. It was going to be a very interesting weekend.

Chapter Ten

It was late when Gennie lounged in an oversized tub filled with hot, fragrant water. The MacGregors, from Daniel down to Mac, were not an early-to-bed group. She liked them—their boisterousness, their contrasts, their obvious and unapologetic unity. And, with the exception of Diana, they had given her a sense of welcome into their family boundaries.

Thinking of Diana now, Gennie frowned and soaped her leg. Perhaps Diana Blade MacGregor was withdrawn by nature. It hadn't taken any insight to see that there was tension between Caine and his wife, and that Diana drew closer into herself because of it, but Gennie felt there had been something more personal in Diana's attitude toward her.

Leave me alone. The signal had been clear as crystal and Gennie had obliged. Not everyone was inherently friendly—not everyone *had* to like her on sight.

Still, it disturbed her that Diana had been neither friendly nor particularly hostile, but simply remote.

Shaking off the mood, she pulled on the old-fashioned chain to let the water drain. Tomorrow, she'd spend some time with her new cousins by marriage, and do as many sketches as she could of the MacGregor home. Perhaps she and Grant would walk along the cliffs, or take a dip in the pool she'd heard was at one of the endless, echoing corridors.

She'd never seen Grant so relaxed for such a long period of time. Oddly, though he was still the remote, arrogant man she'd reluctantly fallen in love with, he'd been comfortable with the numerous, loud MacGregors. In one evening she'd discovered yet something more about him: He enjoyed people, being with them, talking with them—as long as it remained on his terms.

Gennie had caught the tail end of a conversation Grant had been having with Alan after dinner. It had been political, and obviously in depth, which had surprised her. That had surprised her no more, however, than watching him jiggle Serena's baby on his knee while he carried on a debate with Caine involving a controversial trial waging in the Boston courts. Then he had badgered Shelby into a heated argument over the social significance of the afternoon soap opera.

With a shake of her head, Gennie patted her skin dry. Why did a man with such eclectic tastes and opinions live like a recluse? Why did a man obviously at ease in a social situation scare off stray tourists? An enigma.

Gennie slipped into a short silk robe. Yes, he was that, but knowing it and accepting it were entirely different things. The more she learned about him, the more quick peeks she had into the inner man, the more she longed to know.

Patience, just a little more patience, Gennie warned herself as she walked into the adjoining bedroom. The room was huge, the wallpaper old and exquisite. There was an ornate daybed upholstered in rich rose satin and a vanity carved with cupids. It had all the ostentatious charm of the eighteenth century down to the fussy framed embroidery that must have been Anna's work.

Pleasantly tired, Gennie sat on the skirted stool in front of the triple-mirrored vanity and began to brush her hair.

When Grant opened the door, he thought she looked like some fairy princess—part ingenue, part seductress. Her eyes met his in the glass, and she smiled while following through with the last stroke of the brush.

"Take the wrong turn?"

"I took the right one." He closed the door behind him, then flicked the lock.

"Is that so?" Tapping the brush against her palm, Gennie arched a brow. "I thought you had the room down the hall."

"The MacGregors forgot to put something in there." He stood where he was for a moment, pleased just to look at her.

"Oh? What?"

"You." Crossing to her, Grant took the brush from her hand. The scent of her bath drifted through the room. With his eyes on hers in the glass, he began to draw the brush through her hair. "Soft," he murmured. "Everything about you is just too soft to resist."

He could always make her blood heat with his passion, with his demands, but when he was gentle, when his touch was tender, she was defenseless. Her eyes grew wide and cloudy, and remained fixed on his. "Do you want to?" she managed.

There was a slight smile on his face as he continued to sweep the brush through her hair in long, slow strokes. "It wouldn't make any difference, but no, I don't want to resist you, Geneviève. What I want to do..." He followed the path of the brush with his fingers. "Is touch you, taste you, to the absence of everything else. You're not my first obsession," he murmured, with an odd expression in his eyes, "but you're the only one I've been able to touch with my hands, taste with my mouth. You're not the only woman I've loved." He let the brush fall so that his hands were free to dive into her hair. "But you're the only woman I've been in love with."

She knew he spoke no more, no less than the truth. The words filled her with a soaring power. She wanted to share it with him, give back some of the wonder he'd brought to her life. Rising, she turned to face him. "Let me make love to you," she whispered. "Let me try."

The sweetness of the request moved him more than he would have thought possible. But when he reached for her, she put her hands to his chest.

"No." She slid her hands up to his neck, fingers spread. "Let me."

Carefully, watching his face, she began to unbutton his shirt. Her eyes reflected confidence, her fingers were steady, yet she knew she would have to rely on instinct and what he had only begun to teach her. Did you make love to a man as you wanted him to make love to you? She would see.

His wants could be no less than hers, she thought as her fingers skimmed over his skin. Would they be so much different? With a sound that was both of pleasure and approval, she ran her hands down his rib cage, then back up again before she pushed the loosened shirt from his shoulders.

He was lean, almost too lean, but his skin was smooth and tight over his bones. Already it was warming under the passage of her hands. Leaning closer, Gennie pressed her mouth to his heart and felt the quick, unsteady beat. Experimentally, she used the tip of her tongue to moisten. She heard him suck in his breath before the arms around her tightened.

"Gennie..."

"No, I just want to touch you for a little while." She traced the breathless kisses over his chest and listened to the sound of his racing heartbeat.

Grant closed his eyes while the damp, light kisses heated his skin. He fought the urge to drag her to the bed, or to the floor, and tried to find the control she seemed to be asking him for. Her curious fingers roamed, with the uncanny ability to find and exploit weaknesses he'd been unaware he had. All the while she murmured, sighed, promised. Grant wondered if this was the way people quietly lost their sanity.

When she trailed her fingers down slowly to the snap of his jeans, the muscles in his stomach trembled, then contracted. She heard him groan as he lowered his face to the top of her head. Her throat was dry, her palms damp as she loosened the snap. It was as much from uncertainty as the wish to seduce that she loitered over the process.

His briefs ran low at his hips, snug, and to Gennie, fascinatingly soft. In her quest to learn, she touched him and felt the swift convulsive shudder that wracked his body. So much power, she thought, so much strength. Yet she could make him tremble.

"Lie down with me," she whispered, then tilted back her head to look into eyes dark and opaque with need for her. His mouth rushed down to hers, taking as though he were starving. Even as her senses began to swim, the knowledge of her hold over him expanded. She knew what he wanted from her, and she would give it willingly. But she wanted to give much, much more. And she would.

With her hands on either side of his face, she drew him away. His quick, labored breaths fluttered over her face. "Lie down with me," she repeated, and moved to the bed. She waited until he came to her, then urged him down. The old mattress sighed as she knelt beside him. "I love to look at you." Combing the hair back from his temples, she replaced it with her lips.

And so she began, roaming, wandering with a laziness that made him ache. He felt the satin smoothness of her lips, the rustling silkiness of her robe as she slowly seduced him into helplessness. His skin grew damp from the flick and circle of her tongue and his own need. Around him, seeping into the very air he breathed, was the scent she had bathed in. She sighed, then laid her lips on his, nipping and sucking until he heard nothing but the roaring in his own head.

Her body merged with his as she lay down on him and began to do torturous things to his neck with her teeth and tongue. He tried to say her name, but could manage only a groan as his hands—always so sure—fumbled for her.

Her skin was as damp as his and drove him mad as it slid over him, lower and lower so that her lips could taste and her hands enjoy. She'd never known anything so heady as the freedom power and passion gave when joined together. It had a scent—musky, secret—she drew it in. Its flavor was the same, and she devoured it. As her tongue dipped lower, she had the dizzying pleasure of knowing her man was absorbed in her.

He seemed no longer to be breathing, but moaning only. She was unaware that her own sighs of pleasure joined his. How beautifully formed he was, was all she could think. How incredible it was that he belonged to her. She was naked now without having felt him tug off her robe. Gennie knew only that his hands stroked over her shoulders, warm, rough, desperate, then dipped to her breasts in a kind of crazed worship.

How much time passed was unknown. Neither of them heard a clock chime the hour from somewhere deep in the house. Boards settled. Outside a bird—perhaps a nightingale—set up a long, pleading call for a lover. A few harmless clouds blew away from the moon. Neither of them was aware of any sound, any movement outside of that wide, soft bed.

Her mouth found his again, greedy and urgent. Warm breath merged, tongues tangled. Minds clouded. He murmured into her mouth; a husky plea. His hands gripped her hips as if he were falling.

Gennie slid down and took him inside her, then gasped at the rocketing, terrifying thrill. She shuddered, her body flinging back as she peaked instantly then clung, clung desperately to delirium.

He tried to hold on to that last light of reason as she melted against him, spent. But it was too late. She'd stolen his sanity. All that was animal in him clawed to get out. With more of a growl than a groan, he tossed her onto her back and took her like a madman. When she had thought herself drained, she revitalized, filled with him. Her body went wild, matching the power and speed of his. Higher and higher, faster and faster, hot and heady and dark. They rushed from one summit to a steeper one, until sated, they collapsed into each other.

Still joined, with the light still shining beside the bed, they fell asleep.

It was one of those rare, perfect days. The air was mild, just a bit breezy, while the sun was warm and bright. Gennie had nibbled over the casual, come-when-you-want breakfast while Grant had eaten enough for both of them. He'd wandered away, talking vaguely of a poker game, leaving Gennie free to take her sketch pad outdoors alone. Though, as it happened, she had little solitary time.

She wanted a straight-on view of the house first, the same view that could be seen first when traveling up the road. Whether Daniel had planned it that way or not—and she felt he had—it was awesome.

She moved past the thorny rose bushes to sit on the grass near a chestnut tree. For a time it was quiet, with only the sound of gulls, land birds, and waves against rock. The sketch began with rough lines boldly drawn, then, unable to resist, Gennie began to refine it—shading, perfecting. Nearly a half hour had passed before a movement caught her eye. Shelby had come out of a side door while Gennie was concentrating on the tower and was already halfway across the uneven yard.

"Hi. Am I going to bother you?"

"No." Gennie smiled as she let the sketchbook drop into her lap. "I'll spend days sketching here if someone doesn't stop me."

"Fabulous, isn't it?" With a limber kind of grace that made Gennie think of Grant, Shelby sat beside her. She studied the sketch in Gennie's lap. "So's that," she murmured, and she, too, thought of Grant. As a child it had infuriated her that she couldn't match his skill with a pencil or crayon. As they had grown older, envy had turned to pride—almost exclusively. "You and Grant have a lot in common."

Pleased at the idea, Gennie glanced down at her own work. "He has quite a bit of talent, doesn't he? Of course I've only seen one impromptu caricature, but it's so obvious. I wonder...why he's not doing anything with it."

It was a direct probe; they both knew it. The statement also told Shelby that Grant hadn't yet confided in the woman beside her. The woman, Shelby was certain, he was in love with. Impatience warred with loyalty. Why the hell was he being such a stubborn idiot? But the loyalty won. "Grant does pretty much as he pleases. Have you known him long?"

"No, not really. Just a couple of weeks." Idly, she plucked a blade of grass and twirled it between her fingers. "My car broke down during a storm on the road leading to the lighthouse." She chuckled as a perfectly clear image of his scowling face flashed through her mind. "Grant wasn't too pleased to find me on his doorstep."

"You mean he was rude, surly, and impossible," Shelby countered, answering Gennie's grin.

"At the very least."

"Thank God some things are consistent. He's crazy about you."

"I don't know who that shocked more, him or me. Shelby..." She shouldn't pry, Gennie thought, but found she had to know something, anything that might give her a key to the inner man. "What was he like, as a boy?"

Shelby stared up at the clouds that drifted harmlessly overhead. "Grant always liked to go off by himself. Occasionally, when I hounded him, he'd tolerate me. He always liked people, though he looks at them in a rather tilted way. His way," she said with a shrug.

Shelby thought of the security they'd lived with as children, the campaigns, the press. And she thought briefly that with Alan, she had stepped right back into the whirlpool. With a little sigh Gennie didn't understand, Shelby leaned back on her elbows.

"He had a monstrous temper, a firm opinion on what was right and what was wrong—for himself and society in general. They weren't always the same things. Still, for the most part he was easygoing and kind, I suppose, for an older brother."

She was frowning up at the sky still, and remaining silent, Gennie watched her. "Grant has a large capacity for love and kindness," Shelby continued, "but he doles it out sparingly and in his own way. He doesn't like to depend on anyone." She hesitated, then looking at Gennie's calm face and expressive eyes, felt she had to give her something. "We lost our father. Grant was seventeen, between being a boy and being a man. It devastated me, and it wasn't until a long time after that I realized it had done the same to him. We were both there when he was killed."

Gennie closed her eyes, thinking of Grant, remembering Angela. This was something she could understand all too well. The guilt, the grief, the shock that never quite went away. "How was he killed?"

"Grant should tell you about that," Shelby said quietly.

"Yes." Gennie opened her eyes. "He should."

Wanting to dispel the mood, and her own memories, Shelby touched her hand. "You're good for him. I could see that right away. Are you a patient person, Gennie?"

"I'm not sure anymore."

"Don't be too patient," she advised with a smile. "Grant needs someone to give him a good swift punch once in a while. You know, when I first met Alan, I was absolutely determined not to have anything to do with him."

"Sounds familiar."

She chuckled. "And he was absolutely determined I would. He was patient, but—" she grinned at the memory "—not too patient. And I'm not half as nasty as Grant."

Gennie laughed, then flipped over a page and began to sketch Shelby. "How did you meet Alan?"

"Oh, at a party in Washington."

"Is that where you're from?"

"I live in Georgetown—we live in Georgetown," she corrected. "My shop's there, too."

Gennie's brow lifted as she drew the subtle line of Shelby's nose. "What kind of a shop?"

"I'm a potter."

"Really?" Interested, Gennie stopped sketching. "You throw your own clay? Grant never mentioned it."

"He never does," Shelby said dryly.

"There's a bowl in his bedroom," Gennie remembered. "In a henna shade with etched wildflowers. Is that your work?"

"I gave it to him for Christmas a couple of years ago. I didn't know what he'd done with it."

"It catches the light beautifully," Gennie told her, noting that Shelby was both surprised and pleased. "There isn't much else in that lighthouse he even bothers to dust."

"He's a slob," Shelby said fondly. "Do you want to reform him?"

"Not particularly."

"I'm glad. Though I'd hate to have him hear me say it, I like him the way he is." She stretched her arms to the sky. "I'm going to go in and lose a few dollars to Justin. Ever played cards with him?"

"Only once." Gennie grinned. "It was enough."

"I know what you mean," she murmured as she rose. "But I can usually bluff Daniel out of enough to make it worthwhile."

With a last lightning smile, she was off. Thoughtfully, Gennie glanced down at the sketch and sorted through the snatches of information Shelby had given her.

"Frog-faced?" Caine asked when he met Grant in the hall.

"Beauty's in the eye of the beholder," Grant said easily.

With an appreciative grin, Caine leaned against one of the many archways. "You had Dad going. We all got one of his phone calls, telling us the Campbell was in a bad way and it was our duty—he being by way of family—to help him." The grin became wolfish. "You seem to be getting along all right on your own."

Grant acknowledged this with a nod. "The last time I was here, he was trying to match me up with some Judson girl. I didn't want to take any chances."

"Dad's a firm believer in marriage and procreation." Caine's grin faded a bit when he thought of his wife. "It's funny about your Gennie being Diana's cousin."

"A coincidence," Grant murmured, noting the troubled expression. "I haven't seen Diana this morning."

"Neither have I," Caine said wryly, then shrugged. "We disagree on a case she's decided to take." The cloud of trouble crossed his face again. "It's difficult being married and in the same profession, particularly when you look at that profession from different angles."

Grant thought of himself and Gennie. Could two people look at art from more opposing views? "I imagine it is. It seemed to me that Gennie made her uncomfortable."

"Diana had it rough as a kid." Dipping his hands in his pockets, Caine brooded into space. "She's still adjusting to it. I'm sorry."

"You don't have to apologize to me. And Gennie's well able to take care of herself."

"I think I'll take a look for Diana." He pulled himself back, then grinning, jerked his head toward the tower steps. "Justin's on a streak, as usual, if you want to risk it."

Outside, Diana moved around the side of the house and into the front garden before she spotted Gennie. Her first instinct was simply to turn away, but Gennie glanced up. Their eyes met. Stiffly, Diana moved across the grass, but unlike Shelby, she didn't sit. "Good morning."

Gennie gave her an equally cool look. "Good morning. The roses are lovely, aren't they?"

"Yes. They won't last much longer." Diana slipped her hands into the deep pockets of her jade-green slacks. "You're going to paint the house."

"I plan to." On impulse, she held the sketch pad up to her cousin. "What do you think?"

Diana studied it and saw all the things that had first impressed her about the structure—the strength, the fairy-tale aura, the superb charm. It moved her. It made her uncomfortable. Somehow the drawing made a bond between them she wanted to avoid. "You're very talented," she murmured. "Aunt Adelaide always sang your praises."

Gennie laughed despite herself. "Aunt Adelaide wouldn't know a Rubens from a Rembrandt, she only thinks she does." She could have bitten her tongue. This woman, she reminded herself, had been raised by Adelaide, and she had no right denigrating her to someone who might be fond of her. "Have you seen her recently?"

"No," Diana said flatly, and handed Gennie back the sketch.

Annoyed, Gennie shaded her eyes and gave Diana a long, thorough study. Casually, Gennie turned over a page, and as she had done with Shelby, began to sketch her. "You don't like me."

"I don't know you," Diana returned coolly.

"True, which makes your behavior all the more confusing. I thought you would be more like Justin."

Infuriated because the easily spoken words stung, Diana glared down at her. "Justin and I have different ways because we led different lives." Whirling, she took three quick strides away before she stopped herself. Why was she acting like a shrew? she demanded, then placed a hand to her stomach. Diana straightened her shoulders, and turned back.

"I'll apologize for being rude, because Justin's fond of you."

"Oh, thank you very much," Gennie said dryly, though she began to feel a slight stir of compassion at the struggle going on in Diana's eyes. "Why don't you tell me why you feel you have to be rude in the first place?"

"I'm simply not comfortable with the Grandeau end of the family."

"That's a narrow view for an attorney," Gennie mused. "And for a woman who only met me once before when we were what—eight, ten years old?"

"You fit in so perfectly," Diana said before she could think. "Adelaide must have told me a dozen times that I was to watch you and behave as you behaved."

"Adelaide has always been a foolish, self-important woman," Gennie returned.

Diana stared at her. Yes, she knew that—now—she simply hadn't thought anyone else in that part of the family did. "You knew everyone there," she continued, though she was beginning to feel like a fool. "And had your hair tied back in a ribbon that matched your dress. It was mint-green organdy. I didn't even know what organdy was."

Because her sympathies were instantly and fully aroused, Gennie rose. She didn't reach out yet, it wouldn't be welcomed. "I'd heard you were Comanche. I waited through that whole silly party for you to do a war dance. I was terribly disappointed when you didn't."

Diana stared at her again for a full thirty seconds. She felt the desperate urge to weep that was coming over her too often lately. Instead, she found herself laughing. "I wish I'd known how—and had had the courage to do it. Aunt Adelaide would have swooned." She stopped, hesitated, then held out her hand. "I'm glad to meet you again—cousin."

Gennie accepted the hand, then took it one step further and pressed her lips to Diana's cheek. "Perhaps, if you give us a chance, you'll find there are some of the Grandeaus who are almost as human as the MacGregors."

Diana smiled. The feeling of family always overwhelmed her just a little. "Yes, perhaps."

When Diana's smile faded, Gennie followed the direction of her gaze and saw Caine standing among the roses. The tension returned swiftly, but had nothing to do with her. "I need to get a new angle for my sketches," she said easily.

Caine waited until Gennie was some distance away before he went to his wife. "You were up early," he said while his eyes roamed over her face. "You look tired, Diana."

"I'm fine," she said too quickly. "Stop worrying about me," she told him as she turned away.

Frustrated, Caine grabbed her arm. "Damn it, you're tying yourself in knots over that case, and—"

"Will you drop that!" she shouted at him. "I know what I'm doing."

"Maybe," Caine said evenly, too evenly. "The point is, you've never taken on murder one before, and the prosecution has a textbook case built up."

"It's a pity you don't have any more confidence in my capabilities."

"It's not that." Furious, he grabbed her arms and shook. "You know it's not. That's not what this is all about."

His voice grew more frustrated than angry now, while his eyes searched her face for the secrets she was keeping from him. "I thought we'd come farther than this, but you've shut me out. I want to know what it's all about, Diana. I want to know what the hell is wrong with you!"

"I'm pregnant!" she shouted at him, then pressed her hand to her mouth.

Stunned, he released her arms and stared at her. "Pregnant?" Over the wave of shock came a wave of pleasure, so steep, so dizzying, for a moment he couldn't move. "Diana." When he reached for her, she backed away so that pleasure was sliced away by pain. Very deliberately, he put his hands in his pockets. "How long have you known?"

She swallowed and struggled to keep her voice from shaking. "Two weeks."

This time he turned away to stare at the wild roses without seeing them. "Two weeks," he repeated. "You didn't think it necessary to tell me?"

"I didn't know what to do!" The words came out in a rush of nerves and feelings. "We hadn't planned—not yet—and I thought it must be a mistake, but..." She trailed off helplessly as he kept his back to her.

"You've seen a doctor?"

"Yes, of course."

"Of course," he repeated on a humorless laugh. "How far along are you?"

She moistened her lips. "Nearly two months."

Two months, Caine thought. Two months their child had been growing and he hadn't known. "Have you made any plans?"

Plans? she thought wildly. What plans could she make? "I don't know!" She threw her hands up to her face. This wasn't like her, where was her control, her logic? "What kind of a mother would I make?" she demanded as her thoughts poured out into words. "I don't know anything about children, I hardly had a chance to be one."

The pain shimmered through him, very sharp, and very real. He made himself turn to face her. "Diana, are you telling me you don't want the baby?"

Not want? she thought frantically. What did he mean *not want*? It was already real—she could almost feel it in her arms. It scared her to death. "It's part of us," she said jerkily. "How could I not want part of us? It's your baby. I'm carrying your baby and I love it so much already it terrifies me."

"Oh, Diana." He touched her then, gently, his hands on her face. "You've let two weeks go by when we could have been terrified together."

She let out a shuddering sigh. Caine afraid? He was never afraid. "Are you?"

"Yeah." He kissed a teardrop from her cheek. "Yeah, I am. A couple months before Mac was born, Justin told Alan and me how he felt about becoming a father." Smiling, he lifted both her hands and pressed his lips to the palms. "Now I know."

"I've felt so—tied up." Her fingers tightened on his. "I wanted to tell you, but I wasn't sure how you'd feel. It happened so fast—we haven't even finished the house yet, and I thought... I just wasn't sure how you'd feel."

With their hands still joined, he laid them on her stomach. "I love you," he murmured, "both."

"Caine." And his name was muffled against his mouth. "I have so much to learn in only seven months."

"*We* have a lot to learn in seven months," he corrected. "Why don't we go upstairs." He buried his face in her hair and drew in the scent. "Expectant mothers should lie down—" he lifted his head to grin at her "—often."

"With expectant fathers," Diana agreed, laughing when he swept her into his arms. It was going to be all right, she thought. Her family was going to be just perfect.

Gennie watched them disappear into the house. Whatever was between them, she thought with a smile, was apparently resolved.

"What a relief."

Surprised, Gennie turned to see Serena and Justin behind her. Serena carried the baby in a sling that strapped across her breasts. Intrigued by it, Gennie peeped down to see Mac cradled snugly against his mother, sleeping soundly.

"Serena hasn't been able to get close enough to Diana to pry out what was troubling her," Justin put in.

"I don't pry," Serena retorted, then grinned. "Very much. You're sketching the house. May I see?"

Obligingly, Gennie handed over the sketchbook. As Serena studied, Justin took Gennie's hand. "How are you?"

She knew his meaning. The last time she had seen him had been at Angela's funeral. The visit had been brief, unintrusive, and very important to her. In the relatively short time they'd known each other, Justin had become a vital part of her family. "Better," she told him. "Really. I had to get away from the family for a while—and their quiet, continuous concern. It's helped." She thought of Grant and smiled. "A lot of things have helped."

"You're in love with him," Justin stated.

"Now who's prying?" Serena demanded.

"I was making an observation," he countered. "That's entirely different. Does he make you happy?" he asked, then tugged on his wife's hair. "That was prying," he pointed out.

Gennie laughed and stuck her pencil behind her ear. "Yes, he makes me happy—and he makes me unhappy. That's all part of it, isn't it?"

"Oh, yes." Serena leaned her head against her husband's shoulder. She spotted Grant as he came out the front door. "Gennie," she said, laying a hand on her arm. "If he's too slow, as some men are," she added with a meaningful glance at Justin, "I have a coin I'll lend you." At Gennie's baffled look, she chuckled. "Ask me about it sometime."

She hooked her arm through Justin's and wandered away, making the suggestion that they see if anyone was using the pool. Gennie heard him murmur something that had Serena giving a low, delicious laugh.

Family, she thought. It was wonderful to have stumbled on family this way. Her family, and Grant's. There was a bond here that might inch him closer to her. Happy, she ran across the grass to meet him.

He caught her when she breathlessly launched herself into his arms. "What's all this?"

"I love you!" she said on a laugh. "Is there anything else?"

His arms tightened around her. "No."

Chapter Eleven

Gennie's life had always been full of people, a variety of people from all walks of life. But she'd never met anyone quite like the Clan MacGregor. Before the end of the weekend drew near, she felt she'd known them forever. Daniel was loud and blustering and shrewd—and so soft when it came to his family that he threatened to melt. Quite clearly they adored him enough to let him think he tugged their strings.

Anna was as warm and calm as a summer shower. And, Gennie knew intuitively, strong enough to hold her family together in any crisis. She, with the gentlest of touches, led her husband by the nose. And he, with all his shouts and wheezes, knew it.

Of the second generation, she thought Caine and Serena the most alike. Volatile, outspoken, emotional; they had their sire's temperament. Yet when she speculated on Alan, she thought that the serious,

calm exterior he'd inherited from Anna covered a tremendous power...and a temper that might be wicked
when loosed. He'd found a good match in Shelby
Campbell.

The MacGregors had chosen contrasting part-
ners—Justin with his gambler's stillness and secrets,
Diana, reserved and emotional, Shelby, free-wheeling
and clever; they made a fascinating group with interesting eddies and currents.

It didn't take much effort for Gennie to persuade
them to sit for a family sketch.

Though they agreed quickly and unanimously, it
was another matter to settle them. Gennie wanted
them in the throne room, some seated, some standing, and this entailed a great deal of discussion on who
did what.

"I'll hold the baby," Daniel announced, then narrowed his eyes in case anyone wanted to argue the
point. "You can do another next year, lass," he added
to Gennie when there was no opposition, "and I'll be
holding two." He beamed at Diana before he shifted
his look to Shelby. "Or three."

"You should have Dad sitting in his throne—chair,"
Alan amended quickly, giving Gennie one of his rare
grins. "That'd make the clearest statement."

"Exactly." Her eyes danced as she kept her features sober. "And Anna, you'll sit beside him. Perhaps you'd hold your embroidery because it looks so
natural."

"The wives should sit at their husbands' feet,"
Caine said smoothly. "That's natural."

There was general agreement among the men and
definite scorn among the women.

"I think we'll mix that up just a bit—for esthetic purposes," Gennie said dryly over the din that ensued. With the organization and brevity of a drill sergeant, she began arranging them to her liking.

"Alan here..." She took him by the arm and stood him between his parents' chairs. "And Shelby." She nudged Shelby beside him. "Caine, *you* sit on the floor." She tugged on his hand, until grinning, he obliged her. "And Diana—" Caine pulled his wife down on his lap before Gennie could finish. "Yes, that'll do. Justin over here with Rena. And Grant—"

"I'm not—" he began.

"Do as you're told, boy," Daniel bellowed at him, then spoke directly to his grandson. "Leave it to a Campbell to make trouble."

Grumbling, Grant strolled over behind Daniel's chair and scowled down at him. "A fine thing when a Campbell's in a MacGregor family portrait."

"Two Campbells," Shelby reminded her brother with alacrity. "And how is Gennie going to manage to sketch and sit at the same time?"

Even as Gennie glanced at her in surprise, Daniel's voice boomed out. "She'll draw herself in. She's a clever lass."

"All right," she agreed, pleased with the challenge and her inclusion into the family scene. "Now, relax, it won't take terribly long—and it's not like a photo where you have to sit perfectly still." She perched herself on the end of the sofa and began, using the small, portable easel she'd brought with her. "Quite a colorful group," she decided as she chose a pastel charcoal from her box. "We'll have to do this in oils sometime."

"Aye, we'll want one for the gallery, won't we, Anna? A big one." Daniel grinned at the thought, then settled back with the baby in the crook of his arm. "Then Alan'll need his portrait done once he's settled in the White House," he added complacently.

As Gennie sketched, Alan sent his father a mild glance. "It's a little premature to commission that just yet." His arm went around Shelby, and stayed there.

"Hah!" Daniel tickled his grandson's chin.

"Did you always want to paint, Gennie?" Anna asked while she absently pushed the needle through her embroidery.

"Yes, I suppose I did. At least, I can never remember wanting to do anything else."

"Caine wanted to be a doctor," Serena recalled with an innocent smile. "At least, that's what he told all the little girls."

"It was a natural aspiration," Caine defended himself, lifting his hand to his mother's knee while his arm held Diana firmly against him.

"Grant used a different approach," Shelby recalled. "I think he was fourteen when he talked Dee-Dee O'Brian into modeling for him—in the nude."

"That was strictly for the purpose of art," he countered when Gennie lifted a brow at him. "And I was fifteen."

"Life studies are an essential part of any art course," Gennie said as she started to draw again. "I remember one male model in particular—" She broke off as Grant's eyes narrowed. "Ah, that scowl's very natural, Grant, try not to lose it."

"So you draw, do you, boy?" Daniel sent him a speculative look. It interested him particularly because he had yet to wheedle out of either Grant or Shelby how Grant made his living.

"I've been known to."

"An artist, eh?"

"I don't—paint," Grant said as he leaned against Daniel's chair.

"It's a fine thing for a man and a woman to have a common interest," Daniel began in a pontificating voice. "Makes a strong marriage."

"I can't tell you how many times Daniel's assisted me in surgery," Anna put in mildly.

He huffed. "I've washed a few bloody knees in my time with these three."

"And there was the time Rena broke Alan's nose," Caine put in.

"It was supposed to be yours," his sister reminded him.

"That didn't make it hurt any less." Alan shifted his eyes to his sister while his wife snorted unsympathetically.

"Why did Rena break Alan's nose instead of yours?" Diana wanted to know.

"I ducked," Caine told her.

Gennie let them talk around her while she sketched them. Quite a group, she thought again as they argued—and drew almost imperceptibly closer together. Grant said something to Shelby that had her fuming, then laughing. He evaded another probe of Daniel's with a non-answer, then made a particularly apt comment on the press secretary that had Alan roaring with laughter.

All in all, Gennie thought as she chose yet another pastel, he fit in with them as though he'd sprung from the same carton. Witty, social, amenable—yet she

could still see him alone on his cliff, snarling at anyone who happened to make a wrong turn. He'd
changed to suit the situation, but he hadn't lost any of
himself in the process. He was amenable because he
chose to be, and that was that.

With a last glance at what she had done, she looped
her signature into the corner. "Done," she stated, and
turned her work to face the group. "The Mac-
Gregors—and Company."

They surrounded her, laughing, each having a definite opinion on the others' likenesses. Gennie felt a
hand on her shoulder and knew without looking that
it was Grant's. "It's beautiful," he murmured, studying the way she had drawn herself at his side. He bent
over and kissed her ear. "So are you."

Gennie laughed, and the precious feeling of be-
longing stayed with her for days.

September hung poised in Indian summer—a glo-
rious, golden time, when wildflowers still bloomed
and the blueberry bushes flamed red. Gennie painted
hour after hour, discovering all the nooks and cran-
nies of Windy Point. Grant's routine had altered so
subtly he never noticed. He worked shorter hours, but
more intensely. For the first time in years he was
greedy for company. Gennie's company.

She painted, he drew. And then they would come
together. Some nights they spent in the big feather bed
in her cottage, sunk together in the center. Other
mornings they would wake in his lighthouse to the call
of gulls and the crash of waves. Occasionally he would
surprise her by popping up unexpectedly where she
was working, sometimes with a bottle of wine—
sometimes with a bag of potato chips.

Once he'd brought her a handful of wildflowers. She'd been so touched, she'd wept on them until in frustration he had pulled her into the cottage and made love to her.

It was a peaceful time for both of them. Warm days, cool nights, cloudless skies added to the sense of serenity—or perhaps of waiting.

"This is perfect!" Gennie shouted over the motor as Grant's boat cut through the sea. "It feels like we could go all the way to Europe."

He laughed and ruffled her wind-tossed hair. "If you'd mentioned it before, I'd have put in a full tank of gas."

"Oh, don't be practical—imagine it," she insisted. "We could be at sea for days and days."

"And nights." He bent over to catch the lobe of her ear between his teeth. "Full-mooned, shark-infested nights."

She gave a low laugh and slid her hands up his chest. "Who'll protect whom?"

"We Scots are too tough. Sharks probably prefer more tender—" his tongue dipped into her ear "—French delicacies."

With a shiver of pleasure she rested against him and watched the boat plow through the waves.

The sun was sinking low; the wind whipped by, full of salt and sea. But the warmth remained. They skirted around one of the rocky, deserted little islands and watched the gulls flow into the sky. In the distance Gennie could see some of the lobster boats chug their way back to the harbor at Windy Point. The bell buoys clanged with sturdy precision.

Perhaps summer would never really end, she thought, though the days were getting shorter and that morning there'd been a hint of frost. Perhaps they could ride forever, without any responsibilities calling them back, with no vocation nagging. She thought of the showing she'd committed herself to in November. New York was too far away, the gray skies and naked trees of November too distant. For some reason Gennie felt it was of vital importance to think of now, that moment. So much could happen in two months. Hadn't she fallen in love in a fraction of that time?

She'd planned to be back in New Orleans by now. It would be hot and humid there. The streets would be crowded, the traffic thick. The sun would stream through the lacework of her balcony and shoot patterns onto the ground. There was a pang of homesickness. She loved the city—its rich smells, its old-world charm and new-world bustle. Yet she loved it here as well—the stark spaciousness, the jagged cliffs and endless sea.

Grant was here, and that made all the difference. She could give up New Orleans for him, if that was what he wanted. A life here, with him, would be so easy to build. And children...

She thought of the old farmhouse, empty yet waiting within sight of the lighthouse. There would be room for children in the big, airy rooms. She could have a studio on the top floor, and Grant would have his lighthouse when he needed his solitude. When it was time to give a showing, she'd have his hand to hold and maybe those nerves would finally ease. She'd plant flowers—high, bushy geraniums, soft-petaled pansies, and daffodils that would come back and multiply every spring. At night she could listen to the sea and Grant's steady breathing beside her.

"What're you doing, falling asleep?" He bent to kiss the top of her head.

"Just dreaming," she murmured. They were still just dreams. "I don't want the summer to end."

He felt a chill and drew her closer. "It has to sometime. I like the sea in winter."

Would she still be here with him then? he wondered. He wanted her, and yet—he didn't feel he could hold her. He didn't feel he could go with her. His life was so bound up in his need for solitude, he knew he'd lose part of himself if he opened too far. She lived her life in the spotlight. How much would she lose if he asked her to shut it off? How could he ask? And yet the thought of living without her was impossible to contemplate.

Grant told himself he should never have let it come so far. He told himself he wouldn't give back a minute of the time he'd had with her. The tug-of-war went on within him. He'd let her go, he'd lock her in. He'd settle back into his own life. He'd beg her to stay.

As he turned the boat back toward shore, he saw the sun spear into the water. No, summer should never end. But it would.

"You're quiet," Gennie murmured as he cut the engine and let the boat drift against the dock.

"I was thinking." He jumped out to secure the line, then reached for her. "That I can't imagine this place without you."

Gennie started, nearly losing her balance as she stepped onto the pier. "It's—it's nearly become home to me."

He looked down at the hand he held—that beautiful, capable artist's hand. "Tell me about your place in New Orleans," he asked abruptly as they began walking over the shaky wooden boards.

"It's in the French Quarter. I can see Jackson Square from the balcony with the artists' stalls all around and the tourists and students roaming. It's loud." She laughed, remembering. "I've had my studio soundproofed, but sometimes I'll go downstairs so I can just listen to all the people and the music."

They climbed up the rough rocks, and there was no sound but the sea and the gulls. "Sometimes at night, I like to go out and walk, just listen to the music coming out of the doorways." She took a deep breath of the tangy, salty air. "It smells of whiskey and the Mississippi and spice."

"You miss it," he murmured.

"I've been away a long time." They walked toward the lighthouse together. "I went away—maybe ran away—nearly seven months ago. There was too much of Angela there, and I couldn't face it. Strange, I'd gotten through a year, though I'd made certain I was swamped with work. Then I woke up one morning and couldn't bear being there knowing she wasn't—would never be." She sighed. Perhaps it had taken that long for the shock to completely wear off. "When it got to the point where I had to force myself to drive around that city, I knew I needed some distance."

"You'll have to go back," Grant said flatly, "and face it."

"I already have." She waited while he pushed open the door. "Faced it—yes, though I still miss her dreadfully. New Orleans will only be that much more special because I had so much of her there. Places can hold us, I suppose." As they stepped inside she smiled at him. "This one holds you."

"Yes." He thought he could feel winter creeping closer, and drew her against him. "It gives me what I need."

Her lashes lowered so that her eyes were only slits with the green light and glowing. "Do I?"

He crushed his mouth to hers so desperately she was shaken—not by the force, but by the emotion that seemed to explode from him without warning. She yielded because it seemed to be the way for both of them. And when she did, he drew back, struggling for control. She was so small—it was difficult to remember that when she was in his arms. He was cold. And God, he needed her.

"Come upstairs," he murmured.

She went silently, aware that while his touch and his voice were gentle, his mood was volatile. It both intrigued and excited her. The tension in him seemed to grow by leaps and bounds as they climbed toward the bedroom. It's like the first time, she thought, trembling once in anticipation. Or the last.

"Grant…"

"Don't talk." He nudged her onto the bed, then slipped off her shoes. When his hands wanted to rush, to take, he forced them to be slow and easy. Sitting beside her, Grant put them on her shoulders, then ran them down her arms as he touched his mouth to hers.

The kiss was light, almost teasing, but Gennie could feel the rushing, pulsing passion beneath it. His body was tense even as he nibbled, drawing her bottom lip into his mouth, stroking his thumb over her wrists. He wasn't in a gentle mood, yet he strove to be gentle. She could smell the sea on him, and it brought back memories of that first, tumultuous lovemaking on the grass with lightning and thunder. That's what he needed now. And she discovered, as her pulse began to thud under his thumbs, it was what she needed.

Her body didn't melt, but coiled. The sound wasn't a sigh but a moan as she dragged him against her and pressed her open mouth aggressively against his.

Then he was like the lightning, white heat, cold fury as he crushed her beneath him on the bed. His hands went wild, seeking, finding, tugging at her clothes as though he couldn't touch her quickly enough. His control snapped, and in a chain reaction hers followed, until they were tangled together in an embrace that spoke of love's violence.

Demand after unrelenting demand they placed on each other. Fingers pressed, mouths ravaged. Clothes were yanked away in a fury of impatience to possess hot, damp skin. It wasn't enough to touch, they hurried to taste what was smooth and moist and salty from the sea and their mutual passion.

Dark, driving needs, an inferno of wanting; they gave over to both and took from each other. And what was taken was replenished, over and over as they loved with the boundless energy that springs from desperation. Urgent fingers possessed her. An avid mouth conquered him. The command belonged to neither, but to the primitive urges that pounded through them.

Shallow, gasping breaths, skin that trembled to the touch, flavors dark and heated, the scent of the sea and desire—these clouded their minds to leave them victims as well as conquerers. Their eyes met once, and each saw themselves trapped in the other's mind. Then they were moving together, racing toward delirium.

It was barely dawn when she woke. The light was rosy and warm, but there was a faint skim of frost on

the window. Gennie knew immediately she was alone;
touching the sheets beside her, she found them cold.
Her body was sated from a long night of loving but she
sat up and called his name. The simple fact that he was
up before her worried her—she always woke first.

Thinking of his mood the night before, she wasn't
certain whether to frown or smile. His urgency had
never depleted. Time and time again he had turned to
her, and their loving had retained that wild, desperate
flavor. Once, when his hands and mouth had raced
over her—everywhere—she thought he seemed bent
on implanting all that she was onto his mind, as if he
were going away and taking only the memory of her
with him.

Shaking her head, Gennie got out of bed. She was
being foolish; Grant wasn't going anywhere. If he had
gotten up early, it was because he couldn't sleep and
hadn't wanted to disturb her. How she wished he had.

He's only downstairs, she told herself as she stepped
into the hall. He's sitting at the kitchen table having
coffee and waiting for me. But when she reached the
stairwell, she heard the radio, low and indistinct.
Puzzled, she glanced up. The sound was coming from
above her, not below.

Odd, she thought, she hadn't imagined he used the
third floor. He'd never mentioned it. Drawn by her
curiosity, Gennie began the circular climb. The radio
grew louder as she approached, though the news
broadcast was muted and sounded eerily out of place
in the silent lighthouse. Until that moment, she hadn't
realized how completely she had forgotten the outside
world. But for that one weekend at the MacGregors,
her summer had been insular, and bound up in Grant
alone.

She stopped in the doorway of a sun-washed room. It was a studio. He'd cultivated the north light and space. Fleetingly, her gaze skimmed over the racks of newspapers and magazines, the television, and the one sagging couch. No easels, no canvases, but it was the den of an artist.

Grant's back was to her as he sat at his drawing board. She smelled—ink, she realized, and perhaps a trace of glue. The glass-topped cabinet beside him held a variety of organized tools.

An architect? she wondered, confused. No, that didn't fit and surely no architect would resist using his skills on that farmhouse so close at hand. He muttered to himself, hunched over his work. She might have smiled at that if she hadn't been so puzzled. When he moved his hand she saw he held an artist's brush—sable and expensive. And he held it with the ease of long practice.

But he'd said he didn't paint, Gennie remembered, baffled. He didn't appear to be—and what would a painter need with a compass and a T square? One wouldn't paint facing a wall in any case, but...what *was* he doing?

Before she could speak, Grant lifted his head. In the mirror in front of him their eyes met.

He hadn't been able to sleep. He hadn't been able to lie beside her and not want her. Somehow during the night, he'd convinced himself that they had to go their separate ways. And that he could cope with it. She lived in another world, more than in another part of the country. Glamor was part of her life—glamor and crowds and recognition. Simplicity was part of his— simplicity and solitude and anonymity. There was no mixing them.

He'd gotten up in the dark, deluding himself that he could work. After nearly two hours of frustration, he was beginning to succeed. Now she was here, a part of that last portion of himself he'd been determined to keep separate. When she went away, he'd wanted to have at least one sanctuary.

Too intrigued to notice his annoyance, Gennie crossed the room. "What're you doing?" He didn't answer as she came beside him and frowned down at the paper attached to his board. It was crisscrossed with light-blue lines and sectioned. Even when she saw the pen and ink drawings taking shape in the first section, she wasn't certain what she was looking at.

Not a blueprint, surely, she mused. A mechanical...some kind of commercial art perhaps? Fascinated, she bent a bit closer to the first section. Then she recognised the figure.

"Oh! Cartoons." Pleased with the discovery, she inched closer. "Why, I've seen this strip hundreds of times. I love it!" She laughed and pushed the hair back over her shoulder. "You're a cartoonist."

"That's right." He didn't want her to be pleased or impressed. It was simply what he did, and no more. And he knew, if he didn't push her away then, today, he'd never be able to do it again. Deliberately, he set down his brush.

"So this is how you set one of these up," she continued, caught up in the idea, enchanted with it. "These blue lines you've struck on the paper, are they for perspective? How do you come up with something like this seven days a week?"

He didn't want her to understand. If she understood, it would be nearly impossible to push her away.

"It's my job," he said flatly. "I'm busy, Gennie. I work on deadline."

"I'm sorry," she began automatically, then caught the cool, remote look in his eye. It struck her suddenly that he'd kept this from her, this essential part of his life. He hadn't told her—more, had made a point in not telling her. It hurt, she discovered as her initial pleasure faded. It hurt like hell. "Why didn't you tell me?"

He'd known she would ask, but was no longer certain he had the real answer. Instead, he shrugged. "It didn't come up."

"Didn't come up," she repeated quietly, staring at him. "No, I suppose you made certain it didn't. Why?"

Could he explain that it was ingrained habit? Could he tell her the essential truth was that he'd grown so used to keeping it, and nearly everything else, to himself, he had done it without thinking? Then he had continued to do so in automatic defense. If he kept this to himself, he wouldn't have given her everything—because to give her everything terrified him. No, it was too late for explanations. It was time he remembered his policy of not giving them to anyone.

"Why should I have told you?" he countered. "This is my job, it doesn't have anything to do with you."

The color drained dramatically from her face, but as he turned to get off the stool, Grant didn't see. "Nothing to do with me," Gennie echoed in a whisper. "Your work's important to you, isn't it?"

"Of course it is," Grant snapped. "It's what I do. What I am."

"Yes, it would be." She felt the cold flow over her until she was numb from it. "I shared your bed, but not this."

Stung, he whirled back to her. The wounded look in her eyes was the hardest thing he'd ever faced. "What the hell does one have to do with the other? What difference does it make what I do for a living?"

"I wouldn't have cared what you do. I wouldn't have cared if you did nothing at all. You lied to me."

"I never lied to you!" he shouted.

"Perhaps I don't understand the fine line between deception and dishonesty."

"Listen, my work is private. That's the way I want it." The explanation came tumbling out despite him, angry and hot. "I do this because I love to do it, not because I have to, not because I need recognition. Recognition's the last thing I want," he added while his eyes grew darker with temper. "I don't do lectures or workshops or press interviews because I don't want people breathing down my neck. I choose anonymity just as you choose exposure, because it's what works for me. This is my art, this is my life. And I intend to keep it just that way."

"I see." She was stiff from the pain, shattered by the cold. Gennie understood grief well enough to know what she was feeling. "And telling me, sharing this with me, would've equaled exposure. The truth is you didn't trust me. You didn't trust me to keep your precious secret or to respect your precious life-style."

"The truth is our life-styles are completely opposite." The hurt tore at him. He was pushing her away, he could feel it. And even as he pushed he ached to pull her back. "There's no mixing what you need and what I need and coming out whole. It has nothing to do with trust.''

"It always has to do with trust," she countered. He was looking at her now as he had that first time—the angry, remote stranger who wanted nothing more than to be left alone. She was the intruder here as she had been a lifetime ago in a storm. Then, at least, she hadn't loved him.

"You should have understood the word love before you used it, Grant. Or perhaps we should have understood each other's conception of the word." Her voice was steady again, rock steady as it only was when she held herself under rigid control. "To me it means trust and compromise and need. Those things don't apply for you."

"Damn it, don't tell me how I think. Compromise?" he tossed back, pacing the room. "What kind of compromise could we have made? Would you have married me and buried yourself here? Hell, we both know the press would have sniffed you out even if you could've stood it. Would you expect me to live in New Orleans until my work fell apart and I was half mad to get out?"

He whirled back to her, his back to the east window so that the rising sun shot in and shimmered all around him. "How long would it take before someone got curious enough to dig into my life? I have reasons for keeping to myself, damn it, and I don't have to justify them."

"No, you don't." She wouldn't cry, she told herself, because once she began she'd never stop. "But you'll never know the answer to any of those questions, will you? Because you never bothered to share them with me. You didn't share them, and you didn't share the reasons. I suppose that's answer enough.''

She turned and walked from the room and down the long, winding stairs. She didn't start to run until she was outside in the chill of the morning.

Chapter Twelve

Gennie looked at her cards and considered. A nine and an eight. She should play it safe with seventeen; another card would be a foolish risk. Life was full of them, she decided, and signaled the dealer. The four she drew made her smile ironically. Lucky at cards...

What was she doing sitting at a blackjack table at seven-fifteen on a Sunday morning? Well, she thought, it was certainly a convenient way to pass the time. More productive then pacing the floor or beating on a pillow. She'd already tried both of those. Yet somehow, the streak of luck she'd been enjoying for the past hour hadn't lightened her mood. Perversely, she would have preferred it if she'd lost resoundingly. That way, she would have had some new hook to hang her depression on.

Restless, she cashed in her chips and stuffed the winnings in her bag. Maybe she could lose them at the dice table later.

There was only a handful of people in the casino now. A very small elderly lady sat on a stool at a slot machine and systematically fed in quarters. Occasionally Gennie would hear the jingle of coins spill into the tray. Later, the huge, rather elegant room would fill, then Gennie could lose herself in the smoke and noise. But for now, she wandered out to the wide glass wall and looked out at the sea.

Was this why she had come here instead of going home as she had intended? When she had tossed her suitcase and painting gear into the car, her only thought had been to get back to New Orleans and pick up her life again. She'd made the detour almost before she'd been aware of it. Yet now that she was here, had been here for over two weeks, she couldn't bring herself to walk out on that beach. She could look at it, yes, and she could listen. But she couldn't go to it.

Why was she tormenting herself like this? she wondered miserably. Why was she keeping herself within reach of what would always remind her of Grant? Because, she admitted, no matter how many times she'd told herself she had, she had yet to accept the final break. It was just as impossible for her to go back to him as it was for her to walk down to that blue-green water. He'd rejected her, and the hurt of it left her hollow.

I love you, but...

No, she couldn't understand that. Love meant anything was possible. Love meant *making* anything possible. If his love had been real, he'd have understood that, too.

She'd have been better off resisting the urge to look up *Macintosh* in the paper. She wouldn't have seen that ridiculous and poignant strip where Veronica had walked into his life. It had made her laugh, then remembering had made her cry. What right did he have to use her in his work when he wouldn't share himself with her? And he'd used her again and again, in dozens of papers across the country where readers were following Macintosh's growing romance—his over-his-head, dazed-eyed involvement—with the sexy, alluring Veronica.

It was funny, and the touches of satire and cynicism made it funnier. It was human. He'd taken the foolishness and the pitfalls of falling in love and had given them the touch every man or woman who'd ever been there would understand. Each time she read the strip, Gennie could recognize something they'd done or something she'd said, though he had a way of tilting it to an odd angle. With his penchant for privacy, Grant still, vicariously, shared his own emotional roller coaster with the public.

It made her ache to read it day after day. Day after day, she read it.

"Up early, Gennie?"

As a hand touched her shoulder, she turned to Justin. "I've always been a morning person," she evaded, then smiled at him. "I cleaned up at your tables."

He returned the smile, while behind guarded eyes he assessed her. She was pale—still as pale as she had been when she'd so suddenly checked into the Comanche. The pallor only accented the smudges of sleeplessness under her eyes. She had a wounded look that he recognized because he, too, was deeply in love.

Whatever had come between her and Grant had left its mark on her.

"How about some breakfast?" He slipped an arm over her shoulders before she could answer, and began leading her toward his office.

"I'm not really hungry, Justin," she began.

"You haven't really been hungry for two weeks." He guided her through the outer office into his private one, then pushed the button on his elevator. "You're the only cousin I have whom I care about, Genviève. I'm tired of watching you waste away in front of my eyes."

"I'm not!" she said indignantly, then leaned her head against his arm. "There's nothing worse than having someone moping around feeling sorry for themselves, is there?"

"A damned nuisance," he agreed lightly as he drew her into the private car. "How much did you take me for in there?"

It took her a minute to realize he'd changed the subject. "Oh, I don't know—five, six hundred."

"I'll put breakfast on your tab," he said as the doors opened to his and Serena's suite. Her laugh pleased him as much as the hug she gave him.

"Just like a man," Serena stated as she came into the room. "Waltzing in with a beautiful woman at the crack of dawn while the wife stays home and changes the baby." She held a gurgling Mac over her shoulder.

Justin grinned at her. "Nothing worse than a jealous woman."

Lifting her elegant brows, Serena walked over and shifted the baby into his arms. "Your turn," she said, smiling, then collapsed into an armchair. "Mac's teething," she told Gennie. "And not being a terribly good sport about it."

"You are," Justin told her as his son began to soothe sore gums on his shoulder.

Serena grinned, tucked up her feet, and yawned hugely. "I'm assured this, too, shall pass. Have you two eaten?"

"I've just invited Gennie to have some breakfast."

Serena caught her husband's dry look and understood it. Railroaded would have been a more apt word, she imagined. "Good," she said simply, and picked up the phone. "One of the nicest things about living in a hotel is room service."

While Serena ordered breakfast for three, Gennie wandered. She liked this suite of rooms—so full of warmth and color and personality. If it had ever held the aura of a hotel room, it had long since lost it. The baby cooed as Justin sat on the couch to play with him. Serena's low, melodious voice spoke to the kitchen far below.

If you love enough, Gennie thought as she roamed to the window overlooking the beach, if you want enough, you can make a home anywhere. Rena and Justin had. Wherever they decided to live, and in whatever fashion, they were family. It was just that basic.

She knew they worked together to care for their child, to run the casino and hotel. They were a unit. There were rough spots, she was sure. There had to be in any relationship—particularly between two strong-willed personalities. But they got through them because each was willing to bend when it was necessary to bend.

Hadn't she been? New Orleans would have become a place to visit—to see her family, to stir old memories if the need arose. She could have made her home on that rough coast of Maine—for him, with him. She'd have been willing to give so much if only he'd been willing to give in return. Perhaps it wasn't a matter of his being willing. Perhaps Grant had simply not been able to give. That's what she should accept. Once she did, she could finally close the door.

"The ocean's beautiful, isn't it?" Serena said from behind her.

"Yes." Gennie turned her head. "I've gotten used to seeing it. Of course, I've always lived with the river."

"Is that what you're going back to?"

Gennie turned back to the window. "In the end I suppose."

"It's the wrong choice, Gennie."

"Serena," Justin said warningly, but she turned on him with her eyes flashing and her voice low with exasperation.

"Damn it, Justin, she's miserable! There's nothing like a stubborn, pig-headed man to make a woman miserable, is there, Gennie?"

With a half laugh, she dragged a hand through her hair. "No, I don't guess there is."

"That works both ways," Justin reminded her.

"And if the man's pig-headed enough," Serena went on precisely, "it's up to the woman to give him a push."

"He didn't want me," Gennie said in a rush, then stopped. The words hurt, but she could say them. Maybe it was time she did. "Not really, or at any rate not enough. He simply wasn't willing to believe that there were ways we could have worked out whatever problems we had. He won't share—it's as though he's determined not to. It seemed we got close for that short amount of time in spite of him. He didn't want to be in love with me, he doesn't want to depend on anyone."

While she spoke, Justin rose and took Mac into another room. The tinkling music of his mobile drifted out. "Gennie," Justin began when he came back in, "do you know about Grant and Shelby's father?"

She let out a long sigh before she sank into a chair. "I know he died when Grant was about seventeen."

"Was assassinated," Justin corrected, and watched the horror cloud in her eyes. "Senator Robert Campbell. You'd have been a child, but you might remember."

She did, vaguely. The talk, the television coverage, the trial...and Grant had been there. Hadn't Shelby said both she and Grant had been there when their father was killed? Murdered right in front of their eyes. "Oh, God, Justin, it must've been horrible for them."

"Scars don't always heal cleanly," he murmured, touching an absent hand to his own side in a gesture his wife understood. "From what Alan's told me, Shelby carried around that fear and that pain for a long time. I can't imagine it would be any different for Grant. Sometimes..." His gaze drifted to Serena. "You're afraid to get too close, because then you can lose."

Serena went to him to slip her hand into his.

"Don't you see, he kept that from me, too." Gennie grabbed the back of the armchair and squeezed. She hurt for him—for the boy and the man. "He wouldn't confide in me, he wouldn't let me understand. As long as there're secrets, there's distance."

"Don't you believe he loves you?" Serena asked gently.

"Not enough," Gennie said with a violent shake of her head. "I'd starve needing more."

"Shelby called last night," Serena said as the knock on the door announced breakfast. As Justin went to answer she gestured Gennie toward the small dining area in front of the window. "Grant surprised her and Alan with a visit a few days ago."

"Is he—"

"No," Serena interrupted, sitting. "He's back in Maine now. She did say he badgered her with questions. Of course, she didn't have the answer until she spoke to me and found out you were here." Gennie frowned at the sea and said nothing. "She wondered if you were following *Macintosh* in the papers. It took me over two hours to figure why she would have asked that."

Gennie turned back with a speculative look which Serena met blandly. "Perhaps I'm not following you," she said, automatically guarding Grant's secret.

Serena took the pot the waiter placed on the table. "Coffee, Veronica?"

Gennie let out an admiring laugh and nodded her head. "You're very quick, Rena."

"I love puzzles," she corrected, "and the pieces were all there."

"That was the last thing we argued about." Gennie glanced at Justin as he took his seat. After adding cream to her coffee, she simply toyed with the handle of the cup. "All the time we were together, he never told me what he did. Then, when I stumbled across it, he was so angry—as if I had invaded his privacy. I was so pleased. When I thought he simply wasn't doing anything with his talent, I couldn't understand. Then to learn what he was doing—something so clever and demanding..." She trailed off, shaking her head. "He just never let me in."

"Maybe you didn't ask loud enough," Serena suggested.

"If he rejected me again, Rena, I'd fall apart. It's not a matter of pride, really. It's more a matter of strength."

"I've seen you making yourself sick with nerves before a showing," Justin reminded her. "But you always go through with it."

"It's one thing to expose yourself, your feelings to the public, and another to risk them with one person knowing there wouldn't be anything left if he didn't want them. I have a showing coming up in November," she said as she toyed with the eggs on her plate. "That's what I have to concentrate on now."

"Maybe you'd like to glance at this while you eat." Justin slipped the comics section out of the paper the waiter had brought up.

Gennie stared at it, not wanting to see, unable to resist. After a moment she took it from his hand.

The Sunday edition was large and brightly colored. This *Macintosh* was rather drab, however, and lost-looking. In one glance she could see the hues were meant to indicate depression and loneliness. She mused that Grant knew how to immediately engage the readers' attention and guide their mood.

In the first section Macintosh himself was sitting alone, his elbows on his knees, his chin sunk in his hands. No words or captions were needed to project the misery. The readers' sympathies were instantly aroused. Who'd dumped on the poor guy this time?

At a knock on the door he mumbled—it had to be mumbled—"Come in." But he didn't alter his position as Ivan, the Russian emigré, strolled in wearing his usual fanatically American attire—Western, this time, cowboy hat and boots included.

"Hey, Macintosh, I got two tickets for the basketball game. Let's go check out the cheerleaders."

No response.

Ivan pulled up a chair and tipped back his hat. "You can buy the beer, it's an American way of life. We'll take your car."

No response.

"But I'll drive," Ivan said cheeringly, nudging Macintosh with the toe of his pointed boot.

"Oh, hello, Ivan." Macintosh settled back into his gloom again.

"Hey, man, got a problem?"

"Veronica left me."

Ivan crossed one leg over the other and was obviously jiggling his foot. "Oh, yeah? For some other guy, huh?"

"No."

"How come?"

Macintosh never altered positions, and the very absence of action made the point. "Because I was selfish, rude, arrogant, dishonest, stupid, and generally nasty."

Ivan considered the toe of his boot. "Is that all?"

"Yeah."

"Women," Ivan said with a shrug. "Never satisfied."

Gennie read the strip twice, then looked up help-lessly. Without a word, Serena took the paper from her hand and read it herself. She chuckled once, then set it back down.

"Want me to help you pack?"

Where the hell was she? Grant knew he'd go mad if he asked himself the question one more time.

Where the hell was she?

From the lookout deck of his lighthouse he could see for miles. But he couldn't see Gennie. The wind slapped at his face as he stared out to sea and won-dered what in God's name he was going to do.

Forget her? He might occasionally forget to eat or to sleep, but he couldn't forget Gennie. Unfortu-nately, his memory was just as clear on the last ten minutes they had been together. How could he have been such a fool! Oh, it was easy, Grant thought in disgust. He'd had lots of practice.

If he hadn't spent those two days cursing her, and himself, stalking the beach one minute, shut up in his studio the next, he might not have been too late. By the time he'd realized he'd cut out his own heart, she'd been gone. The cottage had been closed up, and the Widow Lawrence knew nothing and was saying less.

He'd flown to New Orleans and searched for her like a madman. Her apartment had been empty—her neighbors hadn't heard a word. Even when he'd lo-cated her grandmother by calling every Grandeau in the phone book, he'd learned nothing more than that Gennie was traveling.

Traveling, he thought. Yes, she was traveling—away from him just as fast as she could. Oh, you deserve it,

Campbell, he berated himself. You deserve to have her skip out of your life without a backward glance.

He'd called the MacGregors—thank God he'd gotten Anna on the phone instead of Daniel. They hadn't heard from her. Not a sound. She might have been anywhere. Nowhere. If it hadn't been for the painting she'd left behind, he might have believed she'd been a mirage after all.

She'd left the painting for him, he remembered, the one she'd finished the afternoon they'd become lovers. But there'd been no note. He'd wanted to fling it off the cliff. He'd hung it in his bedroom. Perhaps it was his sackcloth and ashes, for every time he looked at it, he suffered.

Sooner or later, he promised himself, he'd find her. Her name, her picture would be in the paper. He'd track her down and bring her back.

Bring her back, hell, Grant thought, dragging a hand through his hair. He'd beg, plead, grovel, whatever it took to make her give him another chance. It was her fault, he decided with a quick switch back to fury. *Her* fault, that he was acting like a maniac. He hadn't had a decent night's sleep in over two weeks. And the solitude he'd always prized was threatening to smother him. If he didn't find her soon, he'd lose what was left of his mind.

Infuriated, he swung away from the rail. If he couldn't work, he could go down to the beach. Maybe he'd find some peace there.

Everything looked the same, Gennie thought as she came to the end of the narrow, bumpy road. Though summer had finally surrendered to fall, nothing had really changed. The sea still crashed and roared, eating slowly at the rock. The lighthouse still stood, solitary and strong. It had been foolish for her to have worried that she would find that something important, perhaps essential, had altered since she'd left.

Grant wouldn't have changed, either. On a deep breath she stepped from the car. More than anything, she didn't want him to change what made him uniquely Grant Campbell. She'd fallen in love with the rough exterior, the reluctant sensitivity—yes, even the rudeness. Perhaps she was a fool. She didn't want to change him; all she wanted was his trust.

If she'd misinterpreted that strip—if he turned her away...No, she wasn't going to think about that. She was going to concentrate on putting one foot in front of the other until she faced him again. It was time she stopped being a coward about the things most vital to her life.

As soon as she touched the door handle, Gennie stopped. He wasn't in there. Without knowing how or why, she was absolutely certain of it. The lighthouse was empty. Glancing back, she saw his truck parked in its spot near the farmhouse. Was he out in his boat? she wondered as she started around the side. It was at the dock, swaying gently at low tide.

Then she knew, and wondered she hadn't known from the first. Without hesitation, she started for the cliff.

With his hands in his pockets and the wind tugging at his jacket, Grant walked along the shoreline. So this was loneliness, he thought. He'd lived alone for years without feeling it. It was one more thing to lay at Gennie's feet. How was it possible that one lone female could have changed the essence of his life?

With a calculated effort, he worked himself into a temper. Anger didn't hurt. When he found her—and by God, he would—she'd have a lot to answer for. His life had been moving along exactly as he'd wanted it before she'd barged in on it. Love? Oh, she could talk about love, then disappear just because he'd been an idiot.

He hadn't asked to need her. *She'd* hammered at him until he'd weakened, then she'd taken off the minute he hurt her. Grant turned to the sea, but shut his eyes. God, he had hurt her. He'd seen it on her face, heard it in her voice. How could he ever make up for that? He'd rather have seen anger or tears than that stricken look he'd put in her eyes.

If he went back to New Orleans…she might be there now. He could go back, and if he couldn't find her, he could wait. She had to go back sooner or later; the city meant too much to her. Damn it, what was he doing standing there when he should be on a plane going south?

Grant turned, and stared. Now he was seeing things.

Gennie watched him with a calmness that didn't reveal the thudding of her heart. He'd looked so alone—not in that chosen solitary way he had, but simply lonely. Perhaps she'd imagined it because she wanted to believe he'd been thinking of her. Gathering all her courage, Gennie crossed to him.

"I want to know what you meant by this." She reached in her pocket and pulled out the clipping of his Sunday strip.

He stared at her. He might see things—he might even hear things, but…slowly, he reached out and touched her face. "Gennie?"

Her knees went weak. Resolutely, Gennie stiffened them. She wasn't going to fall into his arms. It would be so easy, and it would solve nothing. "I want to know what this means." She shoved the clipping into his hand.

Off balance, Grant looked down at his work. It hadn't been easy to get that into the papers so quickly. He'd had to pull all the strings at his disposal and work like a maniac himself. If that was what brought her, it had all been worth it.

"It means what it says," he managed, staring at her again. "There's not a lot of subtlety in this particular strip."

She took the paper back from him and stuck it in her pocket. It was something she intended to keep forever. "You've used me rather lavishly in your work recently." She had to tilt back her head in order to keep her eyes level with his. Grant thought she looked more regal than ever. If she turned her thumb down, she could throw him to the lions. "Didn't it occur to you to ask permission first?"

"Artist's privilege." He felt the light spray hit his back, saw it dampen her hair. "Where the hell did you go?" he heard himself demand. "Where the hell have you been?"

Her eyes narrowed. "That's my business, isn't it?"

"Oh, no." He grabbed her arms and shook. "Oh, no, it's not. You're not going to walk out on me."

Gennie set her teeth and waited until he'd stopped shaking her. "If memory serves, you did the walking figuratively before I did it literally."

"All right! I acted like an idiot. You want an apology?" he shouted at her. "I'll give you any kind you want. I'll—'' He broke off, his breath heaving. "Oh God, first."

And his mouth crushed down on hers, his fingers digging into her shoulders. The groan that was wrenched from him was only one more sign of a desperate need. She was here, she was his. He'd never let her go again.

His mind started to clear so that his own thoughts jabbed at him. This wasn't how he wanted to do it. This wasn't the way to make up for what he'd done— or hadn't done. And it wasn't the way to show her how badly he wanted to make her happy.

With an effort, Grant drew her away and dropped his hands to his sides. "I'm sorry," he began stiffly. "I didn't intend to hurt you—not now, not before. If you'd come inside, we could talk."

What was this? she wondered. *Who* was this? She understood the man who had shaken her, shouted at her, the man who had dragged her into his arms full of need and fury. But she had no idea who this man was who was standing in front of her offering a stilted apology. Gennie's brows drew together. She hadn't come all this way to talk to a stranger.

"What the hell's the matter with you?" she demanded. "I'll let you know when you hurt me." She shoved a finger into his chest. "*And* when I want an apology. We'll talk, all right," she added, flinging back her head. "And we'll talk right here."

"What do you want!" In exasperation, Grant threw up his hands. How was a man supposed to crawl properly when someone was kicking at him?

"I'll tell you what I want!" Gennie shouted right back. "I want to know if you want to work this out or sneak back into your hole. You're good at hiding out; if that's what you want to keep doing, just say so."

"I am not hiding out," he said evenly and between his teeth. "I live here because I like it here, because I can work here without having someone knocking on the door or ringing the phone every five minutes."

She gave him a long, level look edged with fury. "That's not what I'm talking about, and you know it."

Yes, he knew it. Frustrated, he stuck his hands in his pockets to keep from shaking her again. "Okay, I kept things from you. I'm used to keeping things to myself, it's habit. And then...And then I kept things from you because the harder I fell in love with you, the more terrified I was. Look, damn it, I didn't want to depend on anyone for—" He broke off to drag a hand through his hair.

"For what?"

"For being there when I needed them," he said on a long breath. Where had that been hiding? he wondered, a great deal more surprised by his words than Gennie was. "I should tell you about my father."

She touched him then, her eyes softening for the first time. "Justin told me."

Grant stiffened instantly and turned away.

"Were you going to keep that from me, too, Grant?"

"I wanted to tell you myself," he managed after a moment. "Explain—make you understand."

"I do understand," she told him. "Enough, at least. We've both lost people we loved very much and depended on in our own ways. It seems to me we've compensated for the loss in our own ways as well. I do understand what it's like to have someone you love die, suddenly, right in front of your eyes."

Grant heard her voice thicken, and turned. He couldn't handle tears now, not when he was so tightly strung himself. "Don't. It's something you have to put aside, never away, but aside. I thought I had, but it crept back up on me when I got involved with you."

She nodded and swallowed. This wasn't the time for tears or a time to dwell on the past. "You wanted me to go that day."

"Maybe—yes." He looked past her to the top of the cliff. "I thought it was the only way for both of us. Maybe it still is; I just can't live with it."

Confused, she put a hand on his arm. "Why do you think being apart might be the best thing?"

"We've chosen to live in two totally different worlds, Gennie, and both of us were content before we met. Now—"

"Now," she said, firing up again. "Now what? Are you still so stubborn you won't consider compromise?"

He looked at her blankly. Why was she talking about compromises when he was about to fold up everything and go with her anywhere. "Compromise?"

"You don't even know the meaning of the word! For someone as clever and astute as you are, you're a closed-minded fool!" Furious, she turned to stalk away.

"Wait." Grant grabbed her arm so quickly, she stumbled back against him. "You're not listening to me. I'll sell the land, give it away if you want. We'll live in New Orleans. Damn it, I'll take out a front page ad declaring myself as *Macintosh*'s artist if it'll make you happy. We can have our picture plastered on every magazine in the country."

"Is that what you think I want?" She'd thought he'd already made her as angry as she was capable of getting a dozen times during their relationship. Nothing had ever compared to this. "You simple, egotistical ass! I don't care whether you write your strip in blood under the cover of darkness. I don't care if you pose for a hundred magazines or snarl at the paparazzi. Sell the land?" she continued while he tried to keep up. "Why in God's name would you do that? Everything's black and white to you. *Compromise!*" Gennie raged at him. "It means give and take. Do you think I care where I live?"

"I don't know!" What little patience he had snapped. "I only know you've lived a certain way—you were happy. You've got roots in New Orleans, family."

"I'll always have roots and family in New Orleans, it doesn't mean I have to be there twelve months out of the year." She dragged both hands through her hair, holding it back from her face a moment as she wondered how such an intelligent man could be so dense. "And yes, I've lived a certain way, and I can live a different way to a point. I couldn't stop being an artist for you because I'd stop being me. I have a show to deal with in November—I need the shows and I need you to be with me. But there are other things I can give back, if you'd only meet me halfway. If I made the ridiculous move of falling in love with you, why would I want you to give up everything you are now?"

He stared at her, willing himself to be calm. Why was she making so much sense and he so little? "What do you want?'' he began, then held up a hand before she could shout at him. "Compromise," he finished.

"More." She lifted her chin, but her eyes were more uncertain than arrogant. "I need you to trust me."

"Gennie." He took her hand and linked fingers. "I do. That's what I've been trying to tell you."

"You haven't been doing a good job of it."

"No." He drew her closer. "Let me try again." He kissed her, telling himself to be gentle and easy with her. But his arms locked and tightened, his mouth hungered. The spray shimmered over both of them as they stood entangled. "You're the whole focus of my world," he murmured. "After you left, I went crazy. I flew down to New Orleans, and—"

"You did?" Stunned, she drew back to look at him. "You went after me?"

"With various purposes in mind," he muttered. "First, I was going to strangle you, then I was going to crawl, then I was going to just drag you back and lock you upstairs."

Smiling, she rested her head on his chest. "And now?"

"Now." He kissed her hair. "We compromise. I'll let you live."

"Good start." With a sigh, she closed her eyes. "I want to watch the sea in winter."

He tilted her face to his. "We will."

"There is something else…"

"Before or after I make love to you?"

Laughing, she pulled away from him. "It better be before. Since you haven't mentioned marriage yet, it falls to me."

"Gennie—"

"No, this is one time we'll do it all my way." She drew out the coin Serena had given her before she'd left the Comanche. "And, in a way, it's a kind of compromise. Heads, we get married. Tails we don't."

Grant grabbed her wrist before she could toss. "You're not going to play games with something like that, Genviève, unless that's a two-headed coin."

She smiled. "It certainly is."

Surprise came first, then his grin. "Toss it. I like the odds."

READERS' COMMENTS ON SILHOUETTE SPECIAL EDITIONS:

"I just finished reading the first six Silhouette Special Edition Books and I had to take the opportunity to write you and tell you how much I enjoyed them. I enjoyed all the authors in this series. Best wishes on your Silhouette Special Editions line and many thanks."

—B.H.*, Jackson, OH

"The Special Editions are really special and I enjoyed them very much! I am looking forward to next month's books."

—R.M.W.*, Melbourne, FL

"I've just finished reading four of your first six Special Editions and I enjoyed them very much. I like the more sensual detail and longer stories. I will look forward each month to your new Special Editions."

—L.S.*, Visalia, CA

"Silhouette Special Editions are — 1.) Superb! 2.) Great! 3.) Delicious! 4.) Fantastic! . . . Did I leave anything out? These are books that an adult woman can read . . . I love them!"

—H.C.*, Monterey Park, CA

*names available on request

Silhouette Desire

Sensual, provocative love stories of modern women in realistic situations.

6 titles every month

All yours, with love, from Silhouette

SD-GEN-1

READERS' COMMENTS ON
SILHOUETTE ROMANCES:

"The best time of my day is when I put my children to bed at naptime and sit down to read a Silhouette Romance. Keep up the good work."

P.M.*, Allegan, MI

"I am very fond of the quality of your Silhouette Romances. They are so real. I have tried to read some of the other romances, but I always come back to Silhouette."

C.S., Mechanicsburg, PA

"I feel that Silhouette Books offer a wider choice and/or variety than any of the other romance books available."

R.R., Aberdeen, WA

"I have enjoyed reading Silhouette Romances for many years now. They are light and refreshing. You can always put yourself in the main characters' place, feeling alive and beautiful."

J.M.K., San Antonio, TX

"My boyfriend always teases me about Silhouette Books. He asks me, how's my love life and naturally I say terrific, but I tell him that there is always room for a little more romance from Silhouette."

F.N., Ontario, Canada

*names available on request

Silhouette Special Edition

COMING NEXT MONTH

THE HEART'S YEARNING—Ginna Gray
When Laura's search for the son she'd had to give up finally ended, she was content to watch him from afar...until Adam Kincaid, her son's adoptive father, unwittingly drew her into a triangle of love.

STAR-CROSSED—Ruth Langan
Fiercely protective Adam London was determined to stop B.J. Conover from writing his mother's biography, but B.J. had a job to do and she couldn't let her growing feelings for Adam stand in her way.

A PERFECT VISION—Monica Barrie
Architect Lea Graham envisioned a community nestled in the New Mexican landscape that Darren Laird was determined to preserve. Could the love that they shared survive a fight to the finish to save their separate dreams?

MEMORIES OF THE HEART—Jean Kent
Was it really possible that foundling Suzy Yoder was the long-lost Hepburn baby, heiress to a vast fortune? Attorney Rich Link had to find the answer, for reasons both legal and personal.

AUTUMN RECKONING—Maggi Charles
Deep in the Berkshire mountains, Marc Bouchard fell in love. Children's-book author Jennifer Bently was more than she'd led him to believe, and her deception threatened the love that they had dared to share.

ODDS AGAINST TOMORROW—Patti Beckman
Every jockey dreams of winning the Kentucky Derby, but for jockey Nikki Cameron the stakes were almost too high. If she triumphed on the bluegrass track, she risked losing the only man she'd ever loved.

AVAILABLE NOW:

ONE MAN'S ART
Nora Roberts

THE CUTTING EDGE
Linda Howard

SECOND GENERATION
Roslyn MacDonald

EARTH AND FIRE
Jennifer West

JUST ANOTHER PRETTY FACE
Elaine Camp

MIDNIGHT SUN
Lisa Jackson